E-Z DICKENS SUPERHERO BOOK FOUR: ON ICE

Cathy McGough

Stratford Living Publishing

WHAT READERS ARE SAYING

FIVE STARS – AMAZON REVIEWER

"After reading part three, I just had to dive into this one. It was so action-packed. I liked the new characters and the unique abilities they brought to the team. It was also great to learn more about the characters from the first part. As in the last part, there were lots of nice details that made me smile. I liked the song with the Furies and the story with the stones. And the epilogue really gave me the feels."

Contents

For Everyday Superheroes.

"You just can't beat the person who never gives up."

Babe Ruth

PROLOGUE

T HE NEXT DAY WAS a school day, but with the end of the world impending neither E-Z nor Lia intended to go.

"I have a very bad feeling," Lia said.

It was breakfast time and she and E-Z were alone. Sam and Samantha were still sleeping, so were the twins Jack and Jill.

"What kind of a bad feeling?" he asked, spooning more cereal into his mouth.

"You know last night, when I thought I heard something?"

"Yes, but you said it was a false alarm. That the sounds went away, and everything went back to normal."

"It did and it didn't. It's difficult to explain. I heard Rosalie calling me, then she stopped. She didn't try again, so I thought everything was fine. But now, I'm worried because I tried to reach her and couldn't. She hasn't responded to any of my texts. I think we should go, and check on her. Just in case. It'll ease my mind to know. Otherwise, I won't be able get anything done today."

"Maybe she's sleeping in? Or her phone battery ran out." He finished his glass of orange juice and backed out from the table. He put the dishes into the dishwasher.

"Maybe. But I still would like to see her."

"Let's go and visit her, to put your mind at ease," he said as he called for a taxi. "I hope they let us in. After all we're not relatives."

They made their way across town and asked about Rosalie at the front desk. The woman asked, "Are you two family?" Both said they weren't. "Take a seat, please," she said.

"See," Lia whispered. "She looked cagey. Like she's hiding something."

"Yeah, I saw that too. But maybe we're imagining it because we're worried about Rosalie. All we can do is wait, and try to keep busy. We're here and we're not budging until we see she's okay."

Thirty minutes later, and they were still waiting. and becoming more restless as time ticked on.

Lia stood up. "I can't wait anymore."

E-Z said, "Whoa! Wait a minute." She sat back down again. "Let's give it another thirty minutes before we go all postal on them."

"What does going postal mean?" Lia asked.

"Oh, I keep forgetting you're not from here. It means to come at something with all your guns blazing. As a last resort. It's a figure of speech of course. Although some postal workers have taken it literally."

"I bet if we were adults, they'd have spoken to us by now. Sometimes I hate being a kid."

"It has its benefits," E-Z said. "Try playing a game on your phone, or reading a book. It'll pass the time and they'll be more helpful to us if we're patient."

"Wish I brought my headphones. I could have listened to Taylor Swift's new tracks."

"Here," he said. "You can borrow mine."

Another thirty minutes went by and E-Z calmly returned to the counter. Lia stayed behind, listening to music. He glanced back. She had her eyes closed. She hadn't even noticed he was gone.

"Uh, any word about when we can see Rosalie?" he asked.

"Sorry, someone is coming out to see you. She knows you're here waiting." The woman clicked at her keyboard. When E-Z didn't moved away she made a second attempt to encourage him to. "I spoke with my Manager personally. She'll be out to speak with you as soon as she can. Please join your friend." She waved her hand in the direction of Lia who was busy on her phone.

E-Z returned to Lia's side, reluctantly. He watched as people milled about. Some were residents, pushing walkers. A few were in wheelchairs, being pushed by attendants while others strummed their wheels themselves. Most residents smiled in his direction, a few waved. He wondered how many of them received regular visitors. He hoped most did.

As the doors opened and closed, the smell of lunch reached his nostrils and his stomach rumbled. He wondered what delicacies the residents were having today. Perhaps fish and chips. Maybe a little pie a la mode. He wished he'd eaten a bigger breakfast when Lia handed back his headphones.

"Any luck speeding things up? I'm starving!"

"Me too and not really. She said the manager will be with us soon, but I don't get why Rosalie just doesn't come on out and see us herself. What's the big deal?"

"I don't feel her presence here," Lia said. "It's like we've been disconnected. The music helped to distract me for a while but now I'm thinking about it again and hungry. Not a good combination."

"I hear you," E-Z said as a tall woman wearing a General Manager's identification badge walked toward them and introduced herself.

"My name is Eleanor Wilkinson and I'm General Manager here." She shook their hands. "I understand you two are friends with Rosalie. Have you visited her here before?"

"No, we haven't been here," Lia said. "But we're friends with her, close friends. And we're worried about her. She didn't reply to my texts, or answer her phone."

Ms. Wilkinson said, "I'm sorry to tell you, but Rosalie died sometime during the night. We're waiting for her next of kin to arrive. They don't live nearby.

"I apologize for keeping you waiting so long. But I needed to speak with them before I spoke to you. You understand. We have policies to follow."

Lia fell back down in the chair and broke into sobs while E-Z took her hand into his and they sat quietly for a few seconds before he asked, "What happened to her?"

"It's under investigation," Wilkinson said. "Sorry, I can't tell you anything more. Unless you're family. I'm sorry for your loss."

"She meant the world to me," Lia said.

"How did you meet her?" Wilkinson asked. "She was a great lady. Loved by all.""We met through a friend," Lia lied.

"Interesting," Wilkinson said, "considering your age difference."

"You mean because I'm a kid and she's not? I mean wasn't" Lia asked angrily. She stood up.

"Sorry, I didn't meant to upset you. Of course, many residents here would love to have friends to chat with. Particularly kids with an interest like yourselves, who they could tell their live stories to. So, they won't be forgotten after they've gone."

"We'll always remember Rosalie," E-Z said.

"Can we see her, to say goodbye?" Lia asked.

"I'm afraid that's out of the question. We have procedures. But if you leave your information, a phone number at the desk we can give you a call. To let you know when the visitation and funeral will be."

E-Z left his phone number at the front desk. They were about to get into a taxi when he remembered the book.

"Wait here," he said. "I'll be right back."

He approached the front desk.

"I'm sorry, but we cannot accept the death of our friend Rosalie. Not unless at least one of us sees her. Ms. Wilkinson said we couldn't go in, but could I just pop my head into the room? I wouldn't stay for long. So, I can tell my friend I've seen Rosalie and I can confirm that she's no longer with us? She's been through so much, with losing her eyes and all. It would ease her mind to know for certain by someone she knows and trusts."

"Ah, poor little thing. I understand. Come with me," the woman said. When she was on the other side of the desk, she asked a colleague to cover for her. "I'll be right back," she said.

E-Z followed her deeper into the heart of the senior citizen's residence. It was bright, not depressing like he'd heard these type of homes could be, but very quiet. Probably because everyone was enjoying lunch in the cafeteria. His stomach rumbled again.

"Everyone is in the dining room," the woman said like she knew what he was thinking. "It's fish and chips day with red jello and whipped cream topping for afters. An immensely popular meal which everyone wants to get in on. Any other day and it would be impossible to let you in because there would be too many people mulling about."

"It sure smells good, " E-Z said. "And thanks for your help, I, we, really appreciate it."

She stopped and pulled the door open.

"This is Rosalie's room. I'll wait here. You've got two minutes or less if anyone spots me."

"Thanks again," E-Z said, as the door swung shut behind him. It smelled odd, like there'd been a bonfire. He looked around the room for cameras. As far as he knew, there weren't any.

Beneath the white sheet their friend was covered from head to toe. He drew nearer, fighting the urge to flee, but needing to know for certain, to see if with his own eyes. He pulled the sheet back and watched as it fell to the floor like a ghost.

Immediately a smell assaulted his nostrils. Like a barbecue. Burned flesh. And he saw Rosalie's arm hanging down, covered in burns and blisters. What had happened to her? Who had done this terrible thing to her, and why?

He pushed his chair away, and looked around the room which was spotless with no sign of a fire. It couldn't have happened here. If not, then where? Did they move her into this room, after?

The woman at the door knocked. "Please hurry!" she said.

He opened her night table drawer. There it was. The book Rosalie had told them about. The one in which she'd recorded the information about the other children.

"Time's up," the woman said.

E-Z stuffed the book behind his back. He pushed the button for the door to open, and they returned to the front desk.

"Thank you," he said. "From my friend and me. You've given us peace. Please let us know when the funeral and visitation will take place. Oh, one more thing, I noticed she, uh, had burns on her body. Were any other residents injured in the fire?"

"Oh my," the woman said. "I don't know. I haven't heard anything about a fire. I haven't seen the body; I mean Rosalie myself. I was only told that she passed. I don't know anything about the details."

"It's okay," E-Z reassured her. "I won't say anything. I appreciate all you've done. Thank you."

"No fire happened here," she said. "No alarm went off that I know of. No fire engines were called. I. Oh my."

E-Z waved and moved away from the counter. The woman was still rambling to herself. He figured it was best for him to get out of there.

The driver helped E-Z get into the back seat alongside of the waiting Lia, then stowed his wheelchair away in the trunk of the vehicle.

"It took you ages," Lia complained. "What's that?"

She tried to grab the book, but E-Z kept a hold of it. He noticed that the fee on the meter was already more money than he had with him.

"It couldn't be helped. I sneaked a peak at Rosalie. And I grabbed this. It's the book she told us about. We'll check it out when we're home." He whispered, "Do you have any money?"

Between the two of them, they didn't have enough to cover the taxi fee.

"You'll have to ask your Mom or Uncle Sam to help us out," he said, as the driver stopped at the house.

The driver helped E-Z back into his chair, while Lia ran inside. She came out with enough money to cover the fare and the driver pulled away.

"Sam gave me the money."

"Did he ask what it was for?"

"No, but I expect he will."

Inside, Sam and Samantha were milling around the kitchen. Trying to hurriedly prepare breakfast while the twins serenaded them with hungry cries.

"Why aren't you in school?" Sam asked.

"I'll explain later. Uh, can we help?"

"No, but thank you," Samantha said. She started feeding Jack.

Sam nodded and set to feeding Jill.

E-Z and Lia went into his room and closed the door. Alfred was reading the newspaper.

"Rosalie is dead," Lia blurted, then she fell to her knees and sobbed, while E-Z put his arm around her and Alfred rushed to her side. The Three hugged together and cried until they had no more tears left.

"What's that you have there?" Alfred asked.

"I grabbed the book."

Lia picked it up, then stood and held it against her chest like she was hugging her friend, instead she saw it all. Rosalie in The White Room. The Furies in The White Room with her. Books burning. Shelves falling. Fire everywhere.

Lia dropped to her knees.

"She was so brave. So very brave."

"You saw the fire?" E-Z asked. "What happened?"

"You knew, about the fire?"

He nodded.

"Why didn't you tell me?" She already knew the answer to the question. He was protecting her from the truth. "When I touched the book, I saw it all. Rosalie was in The White Room. And The Furies were there with her. They wanted her to tell them about us, and the other children. They tortured her, but she didn't give in."

"Why didn't she call us?"

"She tried. I didn't know it was life or death. It went away, so I thought everything was fine."

"It's not your fault," E-Z said.

"She died alone, under the bookshelves, with books burning all around her. She didn't deserve to die like that. No one deserves to die like that." She sobbed into her hands.

"Poor Rosalie," he said. "She could have summoned me. She did it before. Why didn't she summon me?"

"Because she would have put you in danger. She died protecting us."

"So, The Furies tried to get our names and the names of the other children out of her, and she sacrificed herself to save us? To keep our secret. What an amazing woman Rosalie was. We will never forget her - ever," Alfred said as he fought back the tears. "She deserves a medal. A medal of honour."

"Wait a minute, maybe they blocked her from calling us?" E-Z said.

"She did send me an SOS, but she's done that before. One time she did it when they ran out of tea at the home, and she wanted to vent about it. I didn't know this SOS meant her life was in danger."

"You couldn't have known. None of us could. We can't blame ourselves." All three were quiet. "Wait a minute, let's look at the book."

"It's everything she told us it would be. A complete list, with details about all of the kids who are like us. Thank goodness The Furies didn't get their hands on this!"

"Hey, wait a minute!" E-Z said. "The mere idea they tortured her, to find out information about us and the others – means The Furies know all of us exist. That means these kids are out there, all alone and they don't even know what's coming!

"We have to get to them first. Because it's only a matter of time before – however they found out about us, them – figures out where they are."

"What if this is a trap though, for us to lead The Furies directly to them?" Alfred inquired.

"I don't think they know where to find us, otherwise they'd be here, wouldn't they?" E-Z ask. "I mean, they had the element of surprise. By killing Rosalie, they've tipped their hand. Let us know they know something...probably to get in our heads because we're in charge.""What about the other kids?" Lia asked. "How are we going to get to them, without tipping our own hands?"

"Hadz? Reiki?" E-Z called. "If you can hear me, we need your input and your help."

POP.

POP.

"Do you know about Rosalie?" he asked.

"Yes, we do, and it's a sad, sad tale to tell," Hadz said, wiping tears away with her wings. "They tortured here in The White Room. And if that wasn't bad enough – they totally destroyed it and everything in it. All those beautiful, winged books – gone. Rosalie, gone. Gone." She couldn't speak anymore because of the sobs.

"There, there," Reiki said. "And that's not all. We don't know what happened to Rosalie's soul."

"Wait, her body is in the bed in her room across town at the senior's residence. Maybe her soul is there with her?" E-Z asked.

Reiki said, "Do you have anything sealed, closed up, from air, from everything? If yes, please go and fetch it immediately – then we'll go and see if Rosalie's soul is with her. We'll persuade it to go into the container – temporarily – until we figure out where her Soul Catcher is. I sure hope those Furies haven't taken it."

E-Z rushed out into the kitchen, where Sam and Samantha were busy feeding the twins. "Do we still have that big thermos?"

"Yes, it's in the cupboard above the fridge," Sam said, then he cooed to his son.

"Thanks," E-Z said, as he made his way back to his room. "Will this do?"

It took both of them to carry the container.

"Wait!" Alfred cried, just in time to catch them before Hadz and Reiki popped out. "Maybe I can help? I have healing powers. Take me with you. Let me try. Please."

POP

POP

FIZZLE

And the three of them disappeared, landing in Rosalie's room.

"There she is," Alfred said, hopping up on the bed, careful no not to trod on her with his webbed feet. Using his beak, he lifted the sheet, while Hadz and Reiki hovered nearby.

"*What's he going to* do?" Reiki inquired.

"Shhhh," Hadz said.

Alfred placed his beak upon Rosalie's forehead, and touched her heart with one of his wings. Nothing happened.

"Let me try something else," the swan said. This time, he hovered over Rosalie's body, with his forehead pressed up against hers. Again nothing.

"You've tried your best," Hadz said, "now we need to secure her soul. Come out, come out wherever you are."

And just like that, Rosalie's soul drifted toward them.

"You'll be safe in here," Reiki said, as the soul was coaxed into the container, then the lid was firmly closed.

POP.

POP.

FIZZLE.

"Were you able to help her?" Lia asked, but she already knew the answer by the look in Alfred's eyes. She hugged him, "I'm sure you tried your very best."

"He really did," Hadz said.

"Her soul is safe though, here...no one should open it. It needs to be kept secure until the Soul Catcher is ready to take it."

"Perhaps you should keep it with you?" Alfred said. "And thanks for letting me try."

In E-Z's room, *The Three* formulated a plan to bring the other children together. It was decided that E-Z would travel to Australia, for Lachie – also known as The Boy in the Box. Alfred would wing his way to Japan, where he would collect Haruto, the boy who'd been abandoned in the forest. Last, but not least, Lia would travel across the USA to collect Brandy, the girl who could come back to life again.

Their missions were clear – what they'd do when they got there was not. *The Others* were of different ages, diverse cultures, different languages. Some would require permission from their parents, and some would not.

"I wonder what Rosalie told them about us?" Lia asked.

"We can ask them, when we see them," Alfred suggested.

"In the meantime, we have bags to pack and planning to do. I'll make my way there in my chair, but you two have options. Decide what works best for you and put your plan into action. I trust you'll make the right decision and time is ticking."

"I'm glad you said that" Lia said, "because I'm not sure if I want to fly there on a plane. I'm thinking Little Dorrit might be the best option, but I'm not sure if she'll be keen on it. She'll be flying out with one passenger, and coming back with two."

"I'm not sure either," Alfred said. "I could fly there, of my own volition – but, as Haruto is quite young – I'd need to accompany him on the plane – unless his parents came along too. Plus, I have to worry about inclement weather – and it is a long way."

"Like I said, you two decide what works best for you. Alfred, if you decide to fly on a plane – ask Uncle Sam to sort out the details for you."

The Three prepared to bring all of the children together. Then they'd plan – to defeat those wicked Furies. Even if it was the last plan they ever made.

CHAPTER 1
AUSTRALIA

E-Z WAS THE FIRST of the team to leave North America. Flying across the sky in his wheelchair, he enjoyed the freedom which the open air allowed.

The mere idea of putting his wheelchair into storage on a plane gave him the willies. What if it got lost? Or destroyed? It wasn't a risk worth taking. Would Batman abandon his Batmobile? Never.

Although, he was pretty certain he'd have to take a plane back with Lachie. It wouldn't be right to make the kid fly on his own. Maybe they'd make an exception for him and let him fly in his wheelchair? It would be worth inquired. He'd cross that bridge when he got to it. Besides, he didn't want to even THINK about airline food. Thank goodness he had a packed lunch with him now.

He played dodgems with the clouds – and once or twice went straight through them. But he had to focus. After all, Australia was on the other side of the world.

Rosalie's notes about the boy in the box weren't as helpful as he hoped they would be. He'd read about his story on the internet. The thing that stood out the most for him, was that the boy now preferred animals to people. It made sense, after everything he'd been through.

The poor kid was so messed up when they found him, he'd forgotten how to talk. E-Z knew that cruelty existed in the world, but this was unspeakable.

E-Z had lots of questions he hoped to find answers to such as where were Lachie's parents? Who fed and cleaned his cage? Who put him in there? Why?

The article said they sent out reporters to get photos of the boy, to see how he was doing, but the animals wouldn't let them get close. Even when they tried to use a telephoto lens. The magpies attacked and bombarded them. He watched a few clips of magpie attacks – it was like something out the Hitchcock movie *The Birds*. Eventually one of the magpies flew away with a reporter's lens. After that, they left the boy alone.

E-Z hoped he would be able to gain the boy's trust. And that his animal friends would trust him too. If not, his journey would be pointless. Well, not really pointless if he met and spoke to the boy. Would he want to help others, after the way he'd been treated? Only time would tell.

He was flying over the Atlantic Ocean. He'd flown this route before, and it was where he'd met Alfred for the first time. His phone in his pocket vibrated – he had a look and there was a message from Lia.

"Just wanted to let you know that I'm travelling with Little Dorrit."

"You decided not to fly – in a plane – after all?"

"Little Dorrit showed up, and she's on my schedule."

"Sounds like a plan." He sent a thumb's up emoji.

"Where r u?" she asked.

"Just over The Atlantic. Water, water and more water."

They disconnected and he picked up the pace, crossing Africa where he spotted Robben Island – the prison in which they'd held Nelson Mandela for nearly thirty years.

His stomach growled; he didn't fancy the sandwich in his backpack. So, he dropped down in Cape Town and hoped he could use his bank card to get something to eat. He spotted a sign for a place selling "Traditional Fish and Chips" with a British Flag and they accepted bank cards. He carried out his prepared meal, and flew up to the top of Lion's Head. After he completed eating his meal, which was delicious, he took a selfie and then continued his journey.

"Wake me up in two hours," he told his wheelchair which vibrated then sped up. When he woke again, he was crossing the

Indian Ocean. The huge population of stars all around him made him somehow feel less alone. He travelled on, feeling triumphant that he was nearly there when he saw the sun on the horizon pushing its way up the sky to usher in the new day.

Then there it was right in front of him – the spotted the coast of Australia. Excited to see it for himself, he picked up speed and pushed toward it. Realizing he was very thirsty, he reached into his backpacked and pulled out a bottle of water which he drained. He put the empty bottle back in his bag to dispose of later, and although he was still pretty full of the fish and chips he'd eaten earlier. He decided to go ahead and eat the ham and cheese sandwich Uncle Sam had packed.

He flew above Western Australia, now feeling the heat he removed his sweatshirt and put it into his backpack. He continued into The Outback in the Northern Territory wondering where exactly he should land when a tiny bird with feathers of shades of blue accentuated with a black ring around her neck flew toward him.

"Follow me, E-Z," she said. "I've been watching for you."

"Uh, what are you?" he asked.

"I'm a fairy wren," she said. "Come on, he's waiting."

A group of buzzards accompanied them.

"Don't worry," the fairy wren said. "They are our escorts."

He observed the unique form the black-breasted buzzards' white stripes moved in. He'd heard about poetry in motion, now he knew exactly what that phrase meant.

Then he spotted the boy. He was below them, waving. E-Z waved back. Other than the fact that he was sitting on the back of an exceptionally large bird, he looked like any other kid.

"Welcome to Australia," he said. "It'll be dark soon, so follow me. Oh, and by the way, you can call me Lachie."

"Nice to meet you Lachie! I can't wait to see more of your fabulous country. Only wish I could stay longer."

"These are the Savanna Woodlands," the boy said. "Breathe in deeply and you'll notice the scent of the eucalyptus."

"Yes, it smells wonderful," E-Z said.

On they travelled, through stone country, over the floodplains and the billabongs. Finally, they reached their destination in The Outliers.

"This is where I live," the boy said. "Kakadu National Park is Australia's largest terrestrial national park with over 20,000 square kilometers of land. I live here with the plants and animals." The fairy wren landed on his head. "Oh, you're tired again," the boy said with a smile. Then to E-Z, "She often needs a lift."

When they arrived at an area which resembled a campsite, the boy said, "Welcome to my home."

"Thank you," E-Z said. "I could sure use a shower, or bath and I have to pee."

"I dug out a dunny, over there behind the tree. You'll be safe enough. Then I'll show you where the waterfall is, so you can get cleaned up."

"A waterfall, eh? Are there any crocodiles in there?"

"There are crocs about...but they're used to me using the waterfall. I'll come with you for the first time if you'd like?"

"No, I've got wings and so does my chair. We'll fly away if we hear any heavy splashes!"

"Goodo," the youngest said. "Just hover in the falling water - don't land – and you should be fine. Meanwhile I'll gather some food for dinner. If you need help, just shout and I'll come running."

As he neared the waterfall, he noticed signs – and plenty of them with DANGER and WARNING on them. One said there were both saltwater and freshwater crocs about. Yikes.

"Up, to the top!" he directed his chair. He went straight into the water, face first and sat there enjoying it as it fell over and around him. It was cold, at first, but when he got used to it, it felt fine.

As he looked around, he thought about the emu on which the boy met him. It seemed strange a bird of its size – with those enormous wings was unable to fly. He read about birds who couldn't fly online. He was surprised to see kiwis, along with emus, ostriches, penguins, cassowaries, and rheas on the list. He read online that the Ratites DNA had changed so now they can't fly. He felt a little guilty, that he, a boy could fly when those beautiful birds couldn't.

When he was clean and in a new set of clothes, he made his way back to the boy, who was busily preparing their meal.

"This is a billygoat plum."

E-Z took a bite. It tasted amazing.

"This is a red bush apple, and these are black currants."

E-Z ate everything and loved it.

"Now that was our dessert, I need to prepare the main dish." The boy dug and dug, then came up with a pot which was too hot for him to handle. When he removed the lid with a stick, the smell of whatever he'd cooked made E-Z's mouth water.

"These are mussels," the boy said, putting some onto a leaf.

"They are really good. I've never tried mussels before."

The sun was falling out of the sky. "Time to sleep," the boy said.

"Thanks again for making me feel so welcome." E-Z yawned. Until then, he hadn't realized how long he'd been awake.

"You'll sleep up there," he pointed up, into a tree in which there was a treehouse and a rope ladder leading down. "You can fly on up, put on your brake so you won't move about in your sleep. My room's over there," he pointed to another tree with a rope leading down and a treehouse at the top.

"Sleep now," Lachie said. "We'll figure everything out in the morning."

CHAPTER 2
JAPAN

ALFRED COULD HAVE BEEN dropped off by E-Z on his way to Australia. Instead, he decided to fly in the traditional human way – in an airplane.

It took some negotiating on the part of Sam, to convince the airlines to give the trumpeter swan a seat. Let alone one upfront in First Class. Sam used his connections at work, to help Alfred ride in style.

In the cabin wearing headphones and his lucky bow tie, Alfred felt right at home. He was relaxed and the cabin attendant was attentive. Still, he couldn't wait to arrive in Japan. And to meet the boy named Haruto.

Alfred had his backpack stowed nearby and inside he had a few snacks. He'd wait until he was really hungry before digging into his bags of wild rice and wild celery. Along with the food, he had a backup battery for his phone and Sam's credit card with a letter of consent for him to use it.

While he looked out the window as the clouds flew on by, he thought about Haruto. According to Rosalie's notes, he was much younger than the other children. And she had no idea what his powers were – assuming he had powers.

Alfred's plan was to explain everything to Haruto's parents first, and hopefully bring them on board. Then, to ease into more details about how Haruto could help, once he confirmed his area of expertise, i.e., what powers he had.

The difficult part would be convincing them to let their young son travel overseas. Paying wasn't a problem – Sam said he should use his credit card for that. But getting them to agree to let a swan take their child to North America, now that would take some convincing.

He leaned back in the seat and it reclined.

"Would you like anything?" the pretty attendant inquired.

It was a good thing humans could understand him now. It made his life so much easier since no translator was required.

"A cup of tea would hit the spot," Alfred said. "In a bowl," he added. "It's difficult to get this beak into a teacup."

The attendant smiled. Moments later she returned with a bowl, a teabag, sugar, milk, and another bowl of cooler water. "In case the tea is too hot," she said.

"Very thoughtful indeed," Alfred said.

He let the tea cool down, and continued looking out the window. It was so nice to be able to sit back and enjoy the view. Without having to worry about big wind gusts, or snow, or rain, or predators.

Finally, he drank his tea with a little milk and sugar, then dosed off.

He woke up to an announcement that the attendants were preparing passengers for a landing. He'd slept through the entire flight!

Through the window he had a full view of the Haneda Airport. Surrounding it he saw lots and lots of fresh grass for him to eat. He'd sample a little, and save his rice and celery for later.

Further afield, was the outline of the tallest mountain in Japan - Mt. Fuji. Sam had been right, sitting on the left side of the plane was the best place to see what was known as Japan's heart.

"Did you know there is an observation deck, on the fifth floor? You might get a better view of Mount Fuji from there," the attendant said to Alfred.

"I wish I had more time, but thank you. Perhaps on the way back."

The attendants allowed him to exit the plane first. They lined up to say goodbye, like he was a rock star.

Since Alfred only had his carry-on bag and swans don't qualify for passports, he made his way out of the airport to find a taxi.

Before the trip he'd looked online to find out how to hire a taxi in Japan. The information said he should look for a red sticker on the bottom right corner of taxi windshields. This red sticker confirmed the taxi was available to hire.

When he found one with the sticker, he was so happy. He flew up to the open window and gave the driver a note using his beak. The note indicated where he needed to go. The driver was kind, and he didn't mind transporting a swan passenger. He pushed a button on his steering wheel which opened the back door so Alfred could get in. The driver closed the door, and off they went.

Haruto and his family lived in the second largest city in Japan called Yokohama. Although he tried to take in the sights, including the skyline all he could think about was how he was going to convince Haruto and his family to get involved in their fight against The Furies.

The phone in his backpack vibrated. He reached inside; it was a message from E-Z.

"With Lachie now. How r u doing in Japan?"

He typed with his beak, a feat he'd taught himself as he'd been travelling to Japan alone. He was fast too and didn't make many typos.

"Nearly to Yokohama now in a taxi. Hoping to arrive at Haruto's house soon."

E-Z sent him a thumb's up emoji.

Alfred's son had loved to build Gundam robots. In Yokohama, a giant robot was being built. When it was completed, it would stand 59 ft. tall, he discovered as he read about it online. His son would have loved to visit Japan to see it. Since they died, Alfred tried not to think of them as it made him sad. Today though, here in Japan, he decided to see everything he could, like his family was right there with him at his side. Life was too short, even as a swan to be sad all the time.

The driver stopped outside a Garden House with steps with flowers on both sides of the railings. The driver opened his door and Alfred stepped out. He walked up a few stairs, he stopped and snacked on grass which was ample on either side of the staircase. The air was cool and fragrant and the private garden at the front of the house was beautiful. Nearly to the top, he noticed the front area surrounding the house was very inviting, with an owl water feature on the left near the entry. Yet the house itself had all the blinds pulled down like no one was home. He sure hoped someone would be there to greet him. He fancied a snack and a little rest.

He knocked on the door with his beak. A voice emanated from a box near the middle of the door which he couldn't reach without taking flight – which he did.

"My name is Alfred," he said.

The door opened and an elderly woman motioned him inside. He followed her, wondering if one of the team had contacted the family to make introductions in advance of his arrival.

He continued following her, as the sound of his webbed feet slapping down on the hardwood floors were the only sounds heard. The interior of the house was full of wood – and fragrant orchids filled the air. The elderly woman led him to the living area, which was filled with furniture, mostly leather. The blinds in the back of the house were open – he took in the view of plush greenery in the back garden. She pointed toward a chair and he moved to get into it.

He'd only just made himself comfortable when the woman returned to the room with a tray filled with steaming hot tea and some cakes. It was almost like she'd been expecting him – either that or kettles took a lot less time to boil in Japan.

Behind her was a small boy, who held onto her leg and hid behind it. The boy was the right age to be Haruto, but having read that one shouldn't call a Japanese person by their first name without being given permission to. Every now and then the boy glanced at Alfred, then hid again. He looked to be four or five years old at most and was wearing an Optimus Prime t-shirt, short pants, and slippers on his feet.

"You like Optimus Prime?" Alfred asked.

The boy smiled, then returned to his hiding spot.

The woman shooed him away, so she could serve the tea.

Alfred had a translator set up on his phone. He read the words hello on his screen and said, "Kon'nichiwa." He apologized for his poor pronunciation.

"He's British," the boy said, and when he did the older woman tutted.

Alfred was caught by surprise by how well this young boy spoke English. "Ah, you speak English. And yes, I am. You're clever to have noticed my accent."

The boy looked at the woman before speaking this time. She nodded.

"Father and mother are at work," he said. "This is my Sobo" (which translated means Grandmother) "and my name is Haruto."

"Hello," the woman said, also in English. "You should come back, later."

"My name is Alfred. May I call your Haruto?" the boy nodded, then to the woman, "What should I call you?"

"Sobo," she said, "everyone calls me Sobo since I am Haruto's grandmother I am everyone's grandmother. He is happy to share me."

Alfred nodded, "I'm very pleased to meet both of you."

"Did Rosalie send you?" the boy asked.

"You remember Rosalie?" Alfred asked. He was super pleased they had this connection – although knowing in advance Haruto could speak English might have saved him some anxiety. Nevertheless, he decided to follow the woman's advice and rose to leave.

"My father works nearby," Haruto said.

"I need to find somewhere to stay. Can you recommend a place nearby?"

Haruto's grandmother gave Alfred an address with directions on how to get there walking.

"I will call our friend who manages the hotel. He will help you get settled and you can join my son later at the café."

"Thank you," Alfred said.

The walk to the hotel was short and he enjoyed the fresh air. He even sampled some Japanese grass which tasted rather good and took a few sips from fountains too.

The room was small but had everything he needed, and it was exceptionally clean and well kitted out. On his night table was a lamp, with the base in the shape of an owl. He clicked it on and off, noticing how the eyes lit up. He had a shower, changed to a different bowtie, then made his way to the café where he would meet Haruto's father.

His phone buzzed; it was a message from E-Z again.

"How's Japan?"

"Nice," he texted back using his beak to type. "I met Haruto and his grandmother. They speak English. He's very shy, but knew Rosalie. He was noticeably young – maybe four or five. It might be tough to convince his family to let him come to North America."

"Rosalie knew he had powers – but yes, that is younger than I thought he would be," E-Z said. "It's good they speak English. Where are you now?"

"I'm going to a café to meet Haruto's father. By the way, I don't think Rosalie had time to update or complete her notes about Haruto. She referred to him as a baby."

"I'm not sure how concerned we should be at this stage, but I was reading online – it said The Furies can take on any form. Just sharing the info. As we can't recognize them, if they find out about us, we'll need to be careful."

Alfred sent a thumb's up emoji.

"Got to go now," E-Z said.

CHAPTER 3
BAD DREAMS

E-Z WAS ASLEEP AND awake. That is, he could see the ceiling above his bed, feel the mattress supporting his back. And yet, in his head three banshees were shrieking:

"Tell us where you are!"

"Tell us!"

"Tell us NOW!"

"Nooooooooooooooo!" he screamed.

Then above his head on the ceiling was a mirror. But the person in it, being reflected back at him, wasn't himself. Instead, it was his Uncle Sam. And in the reflection his Uncle Sam was screaming and writhing in pain.

"Uncle Sam is in our den!" the first witch shrieked.

"And he'll never get back out again!" the other two chided in unison.

Then the three broke into a kind of laughter, like he'd never heard before. The sounds were hyena-like, guttural, animalistic.

"Speak!" the evil witches demanded and they poked and prodded Uncle Sam like he was a slab of meat being prepared prior to baking.

"E-Z," Uncle Sam said, with his voice shaking like his body was in his reflection. "Whatever they want, don't give it to them. No matter what they do to me, don't give in."

"If you hurt him," E-Z said, "I'll, I'll…"

"Tell us where you are, where they all are, and we'll let him go," they sang together in a voice that wouldn't have seemed out of place in Hades.

"All we need is a clue, or two," the second one said.

"Fill us in on who's who," the first one said.

"Or we'll do away with you know who," the third said.

Then they laughed. Their voices in his head, made it hurt so. But he was only dreaming. He had to wake himself up – NOW.

"Ahhhhhhhhhhhhhhhhhhhhh!" Uncle Sam cried.

More laughter.

E-Z woke up and quickly realized he was in Australia with Lachie, not at home in his own bed. He checked his phone, but only had one bar. He'd keep checking, until he had enough bars to call Uncle Sam. To make sure he was okay. That it had been a nightmare and nothing more.

Below the treehouse, he could hear Lachie moving about. Probably making breakfast. It was good seeing the youngster's life. How he'd put himself back together again after everything he'd been through. Humans were quite remarkable.

Whatever Lachie was cooking smelled good, and his first inclination was to fly right down there and tell him about his nightmare. But something in the back of his mind told him to keep it to himself – for now. After all The Furies couldn't possibly know where he lived. Where they all lived. He checked the bars on his phone again – this time not even one bar. He stuffed it into his pocket and flew down.

"Did you have a nice kip?" Lachie asked, spooning liquid out of a pot sitting over a fire into a bowl.

E-Z accepted it. "I had a weird dream, but otherwise, yes. It's nice up there. Thanks for being so accommodating."

"No worries. There are lots of spirits out here. And unfamiliar sounds to you. If you'd like to talk about the dream, feel free," Lachie said.

"Maybe later."

"Okay, go ahead and dig in. I hope you like mushrooms."

"Love them," E-Z said as he spooned a large amount of the hot steamy soup into his mouth. "It's very good."

"Oh, wait a minute, I forgot the damper – that's bread." He opened some aluminum foil that was in the centre of the firepit and tore it into quarters, giving E-Z the first part.

"This is the best bread I've ever tasted! How'd you learn to cook like this?"

"Some locals taught me. Glad you like it."

They sat quietly, as the sun smiled down on them from high up in the sky. E-Z tried not to think about his nightmare. He pulled the phone out of his pocket and checked the bars again. Just barely one. He loved technology – when it worked.

"Now that your belly is full, let's talk about why you're here," Lachie said. "Most of all, how I can be if assistance."

E-Z didn't speak, instead he glanced at his phone again with a hopeful heart. Lachie didn't seem bothered by it, as he was tearing off another piece of damper. Finally, he pulled himself back together and focused his attention on the matter at hand.

"Sorry, my thoughts were a million miles away."

"That's no problem. Do you want more damper?"

"No, I'm good. So, I'd like to know first of all what Rosalie told you about the three of us. I mean, Alfred, Lia and I."

"Yes, she told me all about the three of you. It was like she was right here with me, telling me a bedtime story. The more she said, the more I wanted to meet you, to help you."

"I'm happy to hear you'd like to help. Let me fill you in on the details first though before you commit. It's not going to be an easy road ahead for any of us."

"I'm not afraid of a challenge," Lachie said. "What did Rosalie tell you about me?"

"To be honest, she didn't tell me much, but I read about you online. Did you ever figure out what happened to your parents?"

"No, and I don't want to. I'm happy here, self-sufficient. I don't need anyone."

"Everyone needs friends," E-Z said.

"Maybe."

"Did Rosalie tell you about The Furies?"

"No, but she said you would be calling upon me one day, when you needed my help to fight evil. And she mentioned The Furies – who I'd already heard of."

"Really? What did you hear?" E-Z inquired.

"The Indigenous people who I learn something new from every time I'm with them, know all about The Furies. They've targeted the originals, trying to punish them, and pushing them off their lands."

"Lachie stood, poured some water onto the fire, and made sure it was fully out.

"I for one, believe evil must exist for good to survive – but there has to be some kind of code – and they don't follow a code.

Anything they do is for their own self-preservation and that's no way to live."

"Those are wise words, for a kid your age," E-Z said. After he said it, he felt a bit embarrassed, like he was trying too hard to be wise being the older of the two. "I think you're probably seven or eight, am I right?"

"I think so, but as to my real age I'm not sure. When they found me, they found no documentation to prove it. Guess when my voice starts changing, I'll have a better idea." He laughed.

"In the meantime, you can choose your own age," E-Z suggested.

"Like I chose my own name," Lachie said. "Anyway, whatever you need me to do, I'm in."

"What's happening with The Furies, is they are using the internet. You know about the internet, yes?"

"I do. They have wi-fi at the library. I love to read. Mythology is pretty cool. Sci-fi too."

"The Furies are using online multiplayer games to entrap the kids. Most kids play games, including me," E-Z said.

"Games are time wasters," Lachie said. "That's what the Indigenous teachers taught me. Life is too short to waste with purposeless distractions."

"Everyone loves games though," E-Z said. "I could give you worldwide figures, but the main thing is, The Furies are taking advantage of this phenomenon. It's like every kid who plays, has given them access to their hearts and minds."

"How so?"

"To level up within the game, you must complete a list of tasks. It's the one way to move ahead in the game. If you didn't do what was asked of you, there'd be no point in playing the game. And yet, what you are being asked to do many times is against the law in real life."

"Against the law! Like what?" Lachie asked.

"Like killing."

Lachie shook his head.

"It's a game, so you do what you need to in order to get to the next level."

"Ok, think I'm getting it. The Furies' mandate was to punish those who committed crimes and went unpunished. They are twisting that mandate, to hurt kids playing an imaginary game."

"That's right Lachie. Exactly. And when the kids die, they steal their souls."

"What for?"

"Have you ever heard of Soul Catchers?"

"No," Lachie said.

"When you die, your soul has a place of eternal rest. It's called a Soul Catcher. But these kids aren't meant to die when the Furies take them, so there's no Soul Catcher waiting for them."

"How do you know all this stuff?" Lachie asked.

"The archangels not only told me, but showed me. I was in my Soul Catcher a few times. They summoned me there. I didn't even know what it was called until all this came up. It's not something humans are supposed to be concerned with. Most think we are going to heaven or hell."

"If your soul catcher was ready, and you're only a kid, why aren't theirs ready?"

"Good question. One I hadn't thought of before. Guess I assumed I was a special circumstance," E-Z said. "But I do know that the archangels screwed something up. Something they won't talk about. Maybe that's why they need our help, to fix this thing."

"How are they doing it though? That's what I don't get."

"They've bent the rules, hoping to take control of all Soul Catchers. When we die, our souls are supposed to go in one that is waiting for us when we die. They're not meant to be transferrable. If they control all of them, then every soul will have nowhere to go. It'll push the afterlife into chaos. So, now that you've heard everything – are you still in?"

"Yes, definitely. Besides, there's nothing better to do out here. I should be an interesting adventure."

"To be one hundred percent honest," E-Z said, "it won't be easy. And you'll be putting your life on the line with the rest of us. But we'll have each other's backs.

"We'll win!"

"I sure hope so, but first, we have to figure out how we're going to get there. Uncle Sam has some airline tickets on-hold for us. What we have to do is pick them up at the nearest international airport. He reserved them."

"No need!" Lachie said. "I have my own transport." He put his two fingers into his mouth and whistled.

For a few minutes nothing happened.

"R---R---R---RRRRRRRRRRRRRRRRR."

"Wh-what was that?" E-Z asked.

Lachie stood very still as the trees shifted and moved in a whisper.

Next E-Z heard wings flapping. From the sound of it, whatever was coming had gigantic wings.

Then the creature broke through the tree foliage. It wouldn't have been out of place in any of the Harry Potter films.

"Is that a dragon?" E-Z inquired.

"He's an Aussiedraco," Lachie said. "Also known as a pterosaur so he's local." To the dragon he said, "G'day mate," and off he went to greet him. The huge scaly creature lowered its head. Lachie petted him, then jumped up onto his back.

"Come on E-Z what are you waiting for?"

"Uh, I have my own transport."

Lachie threw back his head and laughed.

"HAR-HAR-R-R-R-R!"

the creature joined in.

"His name is Baby," Lachie said. "Hop on because Baby wants to take you for a ride, and what Baby wants, Baby gets."

"But my chair!"

Baby reached out his long neck, picked up E-Z. Chair-less he tossed him onto his back. E-Z grabbed onto Lachie as Baby leapt into the air.

"Watch out for the trees!" E-Z cried.

Lachie and Baby laughed.

Off they flew, over miles and miles of red sand.

Soon enough E-Z felt unafraid.

They flew over several rock formations, one which looked like Homer Simpson laying down. Next, they saw Uluru, the huge red monolith.

They spent the entire day, flying across Australia, taking in the sights.

"Better get back," Lachie said. "We need a good night's sleep before we head off to North America and meet the rest of the team."

"Sounds like a plan," E-Z said, now enjoying the ride more and more and wishing it would never end. He wouldn't fall, he had wings if he needed them – but he knew one thing for certain, flying on Baby was the life.

He just wondered where he was going to keep her when they got back home again. The dragon was too big to fit into the garage. He'd manage that problem when he crossed that bridge. Maybe if he and Little Dorrit became friends, they could bunk together?

"Don't worry about me," Baby said.

E-Z did a double take.

"Uh, yes, I can read minds. Not all the time and not everyone's," Baby said. "I'll sort out my own sleeping arrangements. And as to Little Dorrit, well, Unicorns and Dragons don't usually get along – but I'd be willing to give it a go."

Baby dropped them off, and flew away into the night.

E-Z remembered about Uncle Sam, but he was too tired to do anything about it. He'd call him in the morning. Of course, everything would be fine.

CHAPTER 4
OZ DEPARTURE

THE FOLLOWING MORNING WHILE E-Z and Lachie were preparing for their travels, they chatted and got to know each other better.

"I need to recharge my phone and call my Uncle Sam. I'd like to make a pitstop to do both before we leave Australia."

"No problems, as I'd like to pick up a few supplies too. We can do everything at the same time. I'll shop, you can charge your phone and call your Uncle. Anything I should know about?"

"Just a strange dream I had. Makes me want to check on him so I don't worry needlessly."

"Fair enough," Lachie said as he stowed some cooking items away, so they'd be safe until he returned. "I'm sure going to miss this place."

"I know, and your friends too, but you'll be making new ones, and everyone will make you feel right at home. Plus, you'll be back before you know it."

"That's what's worrying me. What if I don't want to come back? What if I get used to having people around? To being spoiled with amenities?" He paused, as two magpies landed, one on each of his shoulders. The birds pecked his ears lightly, like they were whispering to him. Lachie smiled and off they flew.

"What did they say?" E-Z asked.

"Uh, nothing really. They just said they love me, and they are going to miss me." A raven flew down and landed on his shoulder. "This is my mate Erroll."

"Pleased to meet you Erroll," E-Z said. "Uh, how did the two of you become friends?"

Lachie laughed. "Funny you should ask that. Errol's have been around for an exceedingly long time. In fact, his Grandfather, many times over was a pet to someone who might be your distant relative. That's if you're related to Charles Dickens?"

E-Z leaned in, nodding. Lachie definitely had his full attention now.

"Charles Dickens had a pet raven whose name was Grip. According to stories told on down through the years, it was Grip who inspired Edgar Allan Poe to write his most famous poem called The Raven."

"Wow that's so cool!" E-Z exclaimed.

"Birds are super intelligent. As are the Indigenous Elders who took me under their wing when I first arrived in the Outback. They taught me how to read and write, prepare food. They also taught me how to recognize and avoid poisonous flora and fauna.

"I learn something every day from the creatures I meet and talk to. They say that in the old days, everyone could talk to animals – not just me – but something changed. They think it happened in our brains, but whatever happened to everyone else didn't happen to me."

"How did they know you were different?"

"They say they heard about me, when I was born and when I became the boy in the box. Before I was even born, rumours of me were flying around the world in whispers. They'd been waiting for me, that's what they told me for a long time."

"How long?" E-Z inquired.

"I don't want to sound big headed, but they say Mozart knew about me – he had a pet starling and lived in the 17th century. That's more recent. Before him, it can be traced back to Virgil in 70 B.C. Did you know he had a pet fly?"

"Really? A fly – a pet?"

"I've spoken to a bush fly who was related to Virgil – his lame was Leonard, or Leo for short and he confirmed everything." Lachie picked up a pot, and hid it in the bushes, with some other things. "I've also chatted with Andrew Jackson's parrot's relative. Jackson's bird was called Pol – it was a gift for his wife – and was male, but as his relative was female her name was Polly. She had an odd sense of humour!"

"Sounds like it. Uh, I hope we can talk more, but I need to ask you about your special powers – and we should be getting on our way soon, that's if you have everything tucked away safely."

Lachie nodded, "Sure thing. Nearly ready. Just need to secure a few more things. In the meantime, why don't you tell me about yourself first."

"Well, you've already seen me and my chair in action – yes, we can fly. My chair has special powers, besides flying it can also capture criminals and it has a taste for blood. We're a pair, my chair and I, like Batman and his Batmobile."

"Cool!" Lachie said. "But that's kind of weird about the blood thing."

"Waste not want not, don't know who said that but my chair seems to agree. Instead of letting it drip into the ground, it sops it up.

"Our first rescue was a little girl – we saved her from being hit by a vehicle. Then we rescued a plane full of passengers. I don't want to brag and I'm sure you get the gist. Through helping others, I discovered I'm super strong now and so is my chair. Oh, and we've been bullet proofed."

"You mean people have shot at you?"

"Yes, we had a few situations involving guns. Now it's your turn."

My most amazing power is as you've already seen - I can talk to any creatures, any at all. In fact, yesterday when you thought you were talking to Baby, well, you sort of were, but if I wasn't here, she'd be talking gibberish. She communicates to you, through me. I'm like a network, a safety network. I can shut it down or open it up depending on what I decide.

"When I was in that cage, animals used to sit outside and chatter away. Sometimes I thought they were communicating with me, but then, I thought maybe I was going crazy. One time a cockroach flew in through the bars of my cage and said he could help me to get out, if I wanted him to.

"Yuck, I hate cockroaches. Never heard of flying roaches though."

"They're actually pretty smart and have tremendous instinct for survival – I mean they'll eat anything."

"Too bad they didn't eat the people who put you into that box." E-Z thought for a moment. "Why didn't you let him try to rescue you? I mean you didn't have anything to lose."

"What's that old saying, it's better the devil you know?"

"I get that, so you weren't scared of the people who were holding you?"

"It wasn't really a box – it was a cage. But it sounds better if they call it a box. Besides, they never hurt me. They kept me fed and watered. Replaced the newspaper. And I never actually saw who they were since they wore masks."

"I don't get it, why they were keeping you there in the first place."

"That I don't think I'll ever know. And I didn't hang around to get any answers once they let me out."

"How did that go down?"

"They set up a room for me in the same house. Sent along a nice lady, to look after me. I never went outside the house. It was too scary for me."

"Were you able to talk? I mean, if you were in a cage forever, then do you have memories of before? Of your parents?"

"I don't like to talk about it. The past is the past. I can't change it. I always look forward. But I wasn't born in a cage. Sometimes I think I remember going to school. But it could have been a dream. It's difficult to tell the difference between the two some days."

E-Z reminded himself to call Uncle Sam.

"So, how did you end up here, living with animals and one hundred percent self-reliant? I guess you don't miss people?"

"You can't miss what you don't remember. As far as the animals go, I didn't choose them, they chose me. They came to the house, like they knew I wasn't in the cage anymore and they waited for me to come out. They already knew I could talk to them, understand them – but I didn't know I could, until I tried to. Then an entire world opened up for me and I had to be a part of it. I wasn't alone anymore. That's when they offered to take me away and keep me safe. Now you're up to date with the Lachie story."

"It's an amazing story. So, talking to animals. Anything else you've discovered?"

"Well, yes. But it's pretty new."

"Tell me about it."

"It's better if I show you."

"Okay," E-Z said.

He watched as Lachie stood up and walked toward a nearby eucalyptus tree. He was still beside the tree for a second, then stepped forward so he was standing in front of the tree's thick weatherworn trunk. Then he was gone.

"What the?"

Lachie moved to the other side of the tree, then back again against the trunk.

"Oh, so you are invisible?"

"No, look more closely." He stepped away from the tree. "Keep watching my eyes."

E-Z did, and he could see Lachie's eyes in the tree trunk, but he couldn't see Lachie. "Wait a minute," E-Z said. "I get it. It's camouflage – you're a chameleon. Wow!"

Lachie laughed, then returned to his seat.

"How did you discover it? It is a really cool power. You can blend in practically anywhere and no one would ever know!"

"After living with creatures for a while – not seeing any humans – one day a bunch of hikers came through here. I ran to climb up a tree and hide but didn't have enough time – so I just stopped against a tree trunk and stayed still. They walked right by me, like I didn't exist. I couldn't figure it out. A bird landed on my shoulder and a snake crawled up my leg. They could see me, but humans couldn't. That's when I knew I was a chameleon."

"How does it feel? I mean when you go into camouflage mode?"

"It doesn't feel like anything different. It just happens."

"Cool. Well, do you want to know about the rest of the team and what skills they bring to the table?"

Lachie nodded.

"You'll like Lia. She's sighted. Her eyes are in her hands and she can see the now, into some people's minds and she can glimpse the future, what's going to happen sometimes. That part of her power seems to be increasing. Of course, there's the age thing too. When we first met, she was seven and she's twelve now."

"That's really cool,' Lachie said. "And I hear her mother and your Uncle Sam are..."

"Mind if we get going. Just hearing Sam's name makes my anxiety grow again."

"No worries," Lachie said. He whistled and Baby arrived and off they flew to the nearest town, where Lachie picked up a few things, E-Z plugged his phone into the charger and when it was charged enough, he immediately called Sam's number.

There was no answer, instead the call went straight to Sam's voicemail. He tried Samantha's phone and she answered straight away. "Hi, it's E-Z, is Uncle Sam available?"

"Sure E-Z, just a second." Some whispering. "Hi there, kiddo," Sam said. "Where are you now, flying over the ocean yet?"

"Uh just checking that everything is okay with you," E-Z said. "If yes, please say the code word."

"Sponge Bob Square Pants," Uncle Sam said.

"Oh, thank goodness," E-Z said. "I had a weird dream that The Furies had you."

"Ah, we have some friends over and we're just getting ready to sit down and dip some stuff into the fondues. We have chocolate with fruit, cheese and veggies and cheese with bread and meat. It's quite a selection and we have several kinds of wine. The twins are already down for the night."

"Uh, that sounds..."

"Got to go E-Z, see you soon. Keep safe."

"My Uncle is fine, and they are having a fondue – sounds like a bit of a party."

"What's a fondue?" Lachie asked.

"It's a pot where you melt stuff and then you dip other stuff into it. Like dipping strawberries into chocolate and bits of bread into cheese. And you're right, they are married now, and they had twins recently, so the house is pretty full and noisy."

"Ooh, it sounds scrumptious," Lachie said.

With E-Z's phone fully charged, Lachie's supplies safely tucked away on Baby's back, the pair flew out of Australia. They chatted as they went. After hours of seeing nothing of interest, and with stomachs growling they prepared to land for food and bathroom breaks.

"We'll have to land soon to get some lunch anyway – besides, I'm already starving! And congratulations by the way!"

"Thanks! We can stop over in Hawaii for cheeseburgers and fries," E-Z suggested.

"I didn't know Hawaiians specialized in burgers and fries."

"They are part of the USA, so, cheeseburgers and fries – not to mention thick shakes are excellent traditional foods for you to try and I guarantee you, you'll love them."

"I don't eat meat. Cows are people too."

"They have something veggie based, it's still a cheeseburger and you'll love it. Oh, you don't have anything against drinking cow milk, do you?"

"No, I don't."

"Okay chair and Baby - let's go to the nearest cheeseburger joint that serves veggie burgers too," E-Z suggested, as his growling stomach made itself known.

"Onwards!" Lachlan shouted as Baby searched for an appropriate place to land.

CHAPTER 5
BRANDY

LIA AND HER UNICORN travelling companion Little Dorrit, were flying through the clouds.

Lia appreciated her flying companion's graceful but quick movements. Together they invented a game called Jump the Clouds. Depending on the type of cloud, they either jumper over it, under it or through it. Going through it was the most fun.

"I love it when we're inside the cloud," Lia said. "I reach out to touch it, but there's nothing there."

"Looks like the mall below is where we're going," Little Dorrit said before performing a triple jump, going over, then under, then through the same cloud.

"Weeeeeee!" Lia exclaimed.

"Thank you, thank you," the unicorn said, as she pointed downwards.

"Shopping, eh?" Lia said, as she checked it out. It was a large mall, nearly a block long. "I hope I don't need much money, but Mom did give me her credit card in case I needed it."

"Brandy is standing in the aisle of the grocery store, filling up a cart to pass the time. We'd best hurry or her mother will be looking for her soon," the unicorn said.

"That's really cool, you can zero in on her location like that. I can't wait to meet her and to find out more about her powers," Lia said, wrapping her arms around Little Dorrit's neck to prepare for the landing. "I always wanted to have a big sister so this might be my only chance."

"Whistle when you need me," Little Dorrit said, as Lia dismounted, "and I'll meet you right here."

Lia entered the mall through the swinging doors. Straightaway she saw a girl who she hoped was Brandy pushing a trolley in the grocery store. Based upon Rosalie's description it had to be her.

The girl was dressed casually, in a grey hoodie. It was partially zipped, but open enough to reveal an I Love Music red t-shirt which underneath. Her black jeans had musical notes decals on the pockets. Her canvas runners were read to match the t-shirt.

Lia watched the girl for a few moments, before walking toward her. She felt a little intimidated. Like she was meeting a celebrity. In her mind, Brandy oozed style and coolness.

As Lia drew nearer, she imagined they'd be besties one day soon. They'd visit the mall together. Shop for clothes together. Maybe Brandy would even help her to choose some new all-American clothes.

"What are you staring at kid?" Brandy asked in a tone that wasn't very friendly or sisterly. Then in a full swoop she swatted Lia's hands away.

"That's very rude," Lia exclaimed. "Didn't anyone teach you any manners?" She turned her back on the cool girl. She held her breath, counted to ten, then turned to face her again. "Rosalie would be ashamed of you."

"You know Rosalie?"

"Yes, I'm Lia, and I can't see you without my eyes, which are in my hands." Lia raised her arms again.

"Wow!" Brandy exclaimed. "I thought I was weird, but kid, I mean, uh Lia, you take the biscuit." She thrust her hands into her pockets. "But any friend of Rosalie is a friend of mine."

"Uh, thanks," Lia said. "Anywhere we can go to talk?"

"Can't say what you and I would have in common – other than Rosalie," the teenager said as she pushed the trolley onward, leaving Lia behind.

Lia fought back a sob, but managed to get out the words, "We need your help because Rosalie is dead."

Brandy stopped and took a deep breath as a tear trickled down her cheek which she turned and brushed away. "Follow me, kiddo." She abandoned the trolley including all the items in it, and they made their way to a booth just inside the mall and sat down.

"I'll have a glass of water," Lia said. "No ice please."

"Come on kid, live dangerously. She'll have a Root Beer Float – and make that two." After the waitress left, "You'll love it, don't worry. Now, tell me more about why you're here and tell me what happened to that sweet lady Rosalie."

"First, what did Rosalie tell you about me, about us?"

"Nothing. I knew who she was, and I knew she was watching over me. I thought she was an angel at first because she could talk to me inside my head like when I used to pray as a little kid. Then I realized she was a real person, just like me and now she's dead. I'd like to help get the people who killed her – if that's why you're here, then I'm in. Funny, I think she's an angel now, still watching over me."

"Me too," Lia said. "Exactly."

"So, how did it happen?" Brandy asked. "If it's not an insensitive subject to ask about. I always find it's best to talk about the weirdness which makes us who we are. If have my own weirdness, trust me. Everyone does.

"My mom would tell me off for asking you such a personal question. But I like to get to the point. Have you always had eyes on your hands? I'd think you'd be chased by journalists and photographers, people want to talk to you, to hear and tell your story to sell magazines and newspapers."

"Oh, "Lia said, "most people are more interested in celebrity fictional characters, like Harry Potter than they are about real people. If Harry Potter was real, people would avoid him, or tease him. In his world though, he was the hero, so his scar became a part of his story. It made him more human to us, so we could identify with him. But no kid wants to stand out because in this world differences aren't always appreciated.

"It's funny that, how we can relate to and have empathy with fictional characters and not recognize the real heroes in our everyday lives."

"Oh brother," Brandy said, 'you're a bit of a drag, aren't you? It's like talking to a twenty-year-old kid."

"Sorry," Lia said. "I went from seven to ten to twelve, in a short period of time. I didn't get time to adjust."

"That's okay," Brandy said. "And I'd agree with you in principle there, kid, but, since Reality Tv hit the airwaves, we are interested in the lives of ordinary people. That is, ordinary but rich people like the Kardashians. I don't watch it, but millions of people do."

Their drinks arrived. Brandy ate the cherry on the top of hers first, then asked Lia if she wanted hers. When Lia said no, Brandy lifted it off and popped it straight into her gob. "Have a sip. If you try it, you'll definitely like it."

Lia took a big sip through the straw and her face lit up. "It's really good!" Then she stirred the ice cream with the straw as she thought about what to say next.

"For me, I was born with eyes that worked fine. But an accident blinded me, and when I woke up, I had these eyes and I also had what they call the sight. I can see what people are thinking, that's how Rosalie and I first started talking. Time for me isn't like it is for everyone else, but I haven't skipped any years for a while now. Also, as time passes, I sometimes can see what is going to happen to me and to others, you know in the future."

"Did you know Rosalie was going to die before it happened?"

"No, I didn't. It comes and goes. Sometimes it doesn't work at all. It's not one hundred percent reliable. I can't read your mind by the way; in case you're wondering."

"Good. Knowing you could read my mind would be very creepy," Brandy said, taking a huge sip which hit the bottom of the container and made a "that's all folks" sound. "I'd love another one, but I won't," she said. "Best to have moderation, cause if we treat ourselves to the things – things we think we really want all the time then we won't appreciate them as much."

"Very wise," Lia said. "You can have the rest of mine if you want."

"It would be a shame to let it go to waste."

The two girls were quiet for a while until Brandy's phone vibrated. "My mom will be here soon to join us."

"How did she know where we are?"

"Ok, she has her ways, i.e., a tracker on my phone."

"And you don't mind?"

No. I disappeared a few times, but always made it back to the mall. Most of the time when I go, she has no idea. Until I call and ask her to come and pick me up here. That's usually her first clue, my text or call. The app. does save her from worrying about me though. I guess it's not easy having a daughter who can die and come back to life again."

Brandy's mother arrived and introductions were made. They filled her in on Rosalie and Lia's stories, and brought her up to speed on what they'd discussed so far.

"What were you two girls planning?" she asked. "You look like you might be up to no good."

"Just the excess sugar," Brandy said, grinning. "Lia was just about to tell me what they need me for."

"So, you explained about your, reoccurring situation?"

"Briefly. I hadn't gotten to that yet Mom, she only just told me about the accident and why her eyes are on her hands."

The waitress came over and Brandy's Mom ordered a coffee. She returned immediately with a mug, which she filled. "Refills are free," the waitress said. "Just hold up your mug when it's empty, and I'll be right over to fill it up again."

"Thank you," Brandy's Mom said.

"I'd love to hear about it," Lia said, brushing her hair behind her ear. She loved the way Brandy and her mother engaged with each other. They were awfully close; you could tell by the way they kept touching each other. Their closeness made her remember all the times when her mother worked nights and weekends and she had to rely on Hannah her Nanny for everything. It was different now that they were here and her mother was married to Sam, but the new babies sure seemed to take up a lot of her mother's time.

Brandy blurted, "The first time I died, I was little. It was in this very mall. One minute I was dead, the next I was alive again. Like I told you before, I always end up here. That's how much I love this mall."

"That's funny," Lia said.

"I do love shopping!"

"That you do!" Brandy's mother said as her daughter called the waitress back and asked for a glass of ice water.

"Make that two glasses of water," Lia said.

Since she was already there, the waitress refilled Brandy's mother's coffee cup.

Lia felt it was now or never – she should get to the point. It was getting late and Little Dorrit was waiting.

"E-Z, who is our leader is in a wheelchair and he can rescue people, even planes full of passengers. He has super strength and speed, and both he and his wheelchair have wings.

"Alfred is a trumpeter swan, and he has ESP, plus he can bring people and creatures back to life again. Including you there are two more kids we'll be adding to the group, plus E-Z's cousin Charles – so that will make seven of us in all."

"Ah, lucky seven," Brandy's mother said.

Lia continued, "After you've heard everything, if you agree to help us fight The Furies, your life will be in danger. They are three evil sisters – goddesses - who killed Rosalie."

"Evil, eh? Killing Rosalie was a cowardly act! She'd never hurt a fly!" Brandy said.

"Is this information public?" Brandy's mother inquired. "It all sounds so, fictional."

"Why'd they do it?" Brandy asked. "What do they get for killing a sweet old woman like Rosalie?"

"They are using kids. Killing kids," Lia said.

Both Brandy and her mother stopped drinking.

"It's difficult to explain but I'll try my best. When we die, our Souls are are destined for our waiting Soul Catchers – our eternal resting place. Each one of us has our own unique Soul Catcher – so we can never die. Our souls live on. It's not the heaven we imagined, but it is real, and the Furies are killing innocent children – and putting them into Soul Catchers who belong to other people.

"In fact, when Rosalie died, she had nowhere for her soul to go. Fortunately, our friends Hadz and Reiki – they are wannabe angels - were able to capture Rosalie's soul. They're keeping it safe until we eliminate The Furies and put things right again with all the Soul Catchers. Once we eliminate them, the archangels will take over and fix the mess they've caused. Everything will go back to normal again."

"I thought archangels were baddies," Brandy said. "How do we know we can trust them? And why do we want to help them?"

"That's a very big ask of you children," Brandy's mother said.

"It's a very long story. One we can tell you, in time. But right now, we need to get back to headquarters. That's our house. Once we're all under the same roof, we can explain everything and come up with a plan."

"I'm in," Brandy said. "You already had me when you said they killed Rosalie, but now I know they've been killing innocent children too, well let me at them." She raised her glass of water and toasted with Lia.

"Wait," Brandy's mother said, "if the archangels can't beat this thing, then how can they expect you children to..."

"Mom," Brandy patted her hand. "I'm not like other kids. It sounds like we're a bunch of misfits, with special abilities and I'll fit right in. It's not surprising the archangels would ask us to help them.

"Rosalie brought us all together, so we can form a team. If she were here, she'd be with us on the team. Now she's with us in spirit. Together we'll a force to reckon with.

"Besides, we have to make sure Rosalie has her eternal resting place back. Everything happens for a reason, aren't you always the one who tells me that?"

"So, what happens next?" her mother asked.

"We need to be together and E-Z's house is big enough for all of us. The others and Charles Dickens – long story – will be meeting us there."

"Not THE Charles Dickens?"

"The one and only, but he's only ten years old. He arrived and was discovered by two Detectorists in London, England. He's been sent back to earth for a reason. Besides the fact that he and E-Z are cousins. He's one of us. Together we are going to beat those sisters and set the world right again."

"Let's go!" Brandy said. "Mom has my backpack in the car, and it has all the necessaries. I always have a bag packed just in case. It's come in handy quite a few times. I assume the house has a washer and a dryer? Oh, and a hair dryer?"

"Yes, yes and yes," Lia said, then she whistled.

Brandy and her mother covered her ears. "What was that for?"

"Come on outside and I'll introduce you to my friend Little Dorrit – she's a unicorn - and you can grab your bag at the same time." They walked out the doors and she pointed up at the sky, where the unicorn was coming in for a landing.

"Wait a minute," Brandy said, "We're going to be riding across the country on a unicorn?"

Brandy's mother frowned. She felt faint and her legs went all over-cooked spaghetti like.

"Come on over and pet her," Lia said. "Little Dorrit, this is Brandy and her mom."

"Her fur is lovely and soft," Brandy's mother said.

"Would you like a ride to your car?" Little Dorrit asked.

"No, thank you," Brandy's mother said. Then to her daughter, "I don't know how I'm going to explain this to your father. Perhaps you should all come home with me and together we'll explain it and decide if you can go..."

"I have to go," Brandy said. "It's my destiny." She hugged her mother.

"Would it help if you spoke with my mom?" Lia asked, and without waiting for an answer she speeded dialed her, explained the situation and passed her phone over to Brandy's mom who chatted with Samantha then handed the phone back.

Next thing they knew, the three of them were flying around the parking lot, in search of the car with people below honking their horns, taking photos on their phones and bumping into each other with cars and trollies.

"There it is," Brandy's mother said.

Little Dorrit landed, and she slid off. "Wait here and I'll grab my daughter's bag."

She returned, tossed it up to Brandy. "Thanks for the ride," she said to Little Dorrit. To Brandy she said, "Brandy phone home. Daily. Like E.T." She blew her a kiss. Then to Lia, "It was nice to meet you."

"You too," Lia said, as Little Dorrit lifted off the ground. "Don't worry we'll keep your daughter safe."

Brandy's mother watched them fly away, until she could see them no more. By then the nosey parkers had all found something else to look at, so she got into her car and started toward home.

She took the long way home. She needed to think how she was going to explain it all to Brandy's father.

CHAPTER 6

HARUTO

ALFRED WAITED AT THE front of the café until the owner, who'd been expecting a new customer. Haruto's grandmother failed to mention the customer was a trumpeter swan. When the owner saw Alfred, he took him to a table way in the back.

Alfred didn't mind being out of the way. In fact, he preferred it since there was a sign which indicated no pets – not that swans were considered pets in Japan or anywhere else in the world he knew of.

As he sat quietly, waiting for Haruto's father to arrive, he used the Café's free WI-FI and discovered some really cool things about Japan's Café Cultures. Like in Yokohama, there were cafes for cat lovers and one in celebration of hedgehogs.

Fifteen minutes later a man entered the café. Alfred knew it was Haruto's father immediately, as the made advanced quickly toward his table.

"Naze watashitachiha daidokoro no chikaku ni iru nodesu ka?" he asked the owner of the café (which translated means: why are we near the kitchen?"

"Kare wa hakuchōdakara!" the owner said before he moved away from the table (which translated means: Because he's a swan!)

When he returned a few minutes later with a tray filled with Bubble Tea, the owner said, " Mōshiwakearimasen" (which translated means, I'm sorry.)

" Ī nda yo," Haruto's father said with a smile (which translated means: It's okay.)

Alfred's tea was served in a bowl big enough for him to stick his beak into. His tea was iced – good thing as he didn't want to burn his tongue or wait a long time for it to cool down.

"Domo arigato gozaimasu," Alfred said (which translated means: thank you very much.)

"Iie," Haruto's father replied (which translated means: don't mention it.)

They sat quietly, eyeing each other while sipping their teas for a while.

"Why are you here?" Haruto's father asked abruptly. "My wife is afraid you want to take our son from us, and you can't have him. Yes, we found him but we're the only parents he has ever known."

"Whoa!" Alfred exclaimed. "Nothing will happen unless you want it to. By the way, your son's English is excellent," Alfred said. "As is your own."

"Flattery will do you no good here. As I said before, you can't have my son."

"If Haruto could help us, to save the world? Would you still say no?"

"Haruto is just a boy. You're a swan. What can boys and swans do that men can't do? You can't have him." He crossed his arms.

"What if we can't save the world, without his help? What if he wants to help us?"

"Haruto doesn't know anything of life. He can't help you. Find someone else's son, someone older. Someone who has been born to save the world. Not a boy. Not my boy, Haruto. Not today, tomorrow or ever."

"What if we let him decide?" Alfred said. "After I explain everything that is."

"Tell me everything now. And I will decide what he should know. But first, let me ask you - what makes you think a little boy like my son can help you?"

"We think, like the rest of us, he has gifts, unique gifts. He's not like other children, is he? When Rosalie mentioned him, he was still a baby. Has he aged more quickly than other children?"

Haruto's father shook his head. "When we found him five years ago, he was a baby. He has grown, like any child grows."

"Oh, sorry. Rosalie didn't have time to update or complete her notes. Still, don't you want your son to be with other children who are gifted like him? He'd be one of us, accepted by us. And we'd honour his gifts and protect him."

"Are you suggesting that I cannot protect my own son?"

"No, Sir. I'm not saying that at all. I'm saying telling you that we need him and maybe, just maybe, he needs us. A boy who stands alone can never be as strong as a boy who is a member of a team."

"Perhaps he is lonely. Perhaps, but he is young, and he'll grow out of it." Haruto's father remained quiet before he asked, "What is your gift and who is the enemy?"

"I have healing powers, for humans and animals – mostly the latter. I can read minds. Lia can see into the future. E-Z saves lives. am able to heal the sick and read minds. We even have a Superhero website, which I can show you if you'd like to see everything for yourself as proof."

"I already saw your website," Haruto's father said. "You are known as *The Three*. Aren't three of you powerful enough to take on whatever enemies you come up against? How can a little boy like Haruto help you? He can hardly remember to brush his teeth."

"I get that. I had a son too when I was human."

"You were human once? What happened to your son?"

"They died, and I was made into a swan. It's a long-complicated story. Main thing is, until recently we didn't know there were other children. It was Rosalie. She was an amazing lady, with the ability to communicate with children in her mind. She spoke with Lia, Haruto, Brandy and Lachie. She brought everyone together and paid a high price for it. The Furies killed her when she wouldn't reveal any information about the children to them. Without Rosalie, we wouldn't know the other existed and we wouldn't be here wanting to protect your son, or asking for his help in defeating those evil sisters.

"I was sent to speak with Haruto and to explain what we're up against. Of course, he can refuse, you can refuse for him – but without him we may not be able to overcome the evil goddesses known as The Furies."

The owner offered more tea. Alfred declined, however Haruto's father's hands trembled slightly as he lifted his newly refilled tea and sipped.

"Is Haruto the youngest child?"

Alfred nodded.

"Tell me about the other two new recruits."

"Brandy dies, and is reborn. Lachie can speak and be understood by all creatures."

"This Brandy is reborn as herself each time?" Haruto's father asked.

"That's my understanding."

"How old is she?"

"That I do not know for certain, but I believe she's a teenager. Why does it matter?" Alfred asked.

"Because being reborn repeatedly while remaining in the human state means Brandy is stuck in the Learning stage. Therefore, she will do well with others who are more advanced than her. She will learn from them and perhaps, it will help her to attain the next stage."

Alfred understood, somewhat, but didn't say anything.

"My son would not advance Brandy's life, therefore I will not permit him to be a part of this fight. I'm sorry for wasting your time."

"Well, I've come all this way – so, what will it hurt for me to talk to him, with you, your wife and mother present. Give him the choice. Let him decide. If it's not right for him, if you think he's too young or unprepared – we will understand – but please at least let's talk to him about it. See how much he can understand. Let him be the one who says no – then I will get back on the plane and you'll never see me again."

"You are a swan, and you fly on a plane?" he laughed, loudly. Other patrons of the café joined in although they had no idea why he was laughing. They laughed because the sound of Haruto's father's laughter was infectious.

"Tell me what your team is intending to do and why. Then I will decide. If you can convince me, then perhaps I will let you try to convince Haruto."

"When we die, our souls leave our bodies, and go to their eternal rest in what is called a Soul Catcher. I know this is different from what we believe, but it is true. The Furies have been killing children – children who are playing computer games – and then putting their souls into Soul Catchers meant for other souls. When others die, there is nowhere for their Souls to go."

Haruto's father was quiet for a few moments.

"If he wants to, my son, Haruto will help. He will tell you what his talent is. He will tell you what he wants you to know, and he will decide."

"Thank you," Alfred said.

They stood, left the café, and made their way to Haruto's home. When they arrived, dinner was served immediately, and everyone was brought up to speed regarding the mission.

"What happens to the other souls? If they have nowhere to go?" Haruto asked, putting down his chopsticks and taking a sip of water.

"That we don't know for certain," Alfred replied. He glanced at Haruto's father who nodded. "But Rosalie. Do you remember Rosalie?"

"Yes, I knew her, and I know that she died," Haruto said. He sat up very straight, "Do you mean her soul has no home? How can I help her to reach her home?"

"I'm glad you want to help, Haruto," Alfred said. "Rosalie's soul is safely held by two wannabe angels who have helped us and E-Z, in the past. So, she's all good for now.

"Before I explain more, I'm curious you're your special powers you possess?"

Haruto stood, looked at his father, who nodded, then said. "I move very fast." And he began to twirl, faster and faster and faster until he disappeared.

"Whoa!" Alfred said. "You're like a disappearing version of the Tasmanian Devil!"

"We never grow tired of seeing him in action," his mother said. She'd been noticeably quiet up until that comment. "Come back now, child," she said. "Come back."

He arrived in the same way he'd disappeared, only they couldn't see him twirling this time until he reappeared. "I'm hungry again!" Haruto exclaimed. And he sat down, refilled his plate and ate ravenously.

"Does it always make you hungry?" Alfred asked.

"Always," Sobo said, offering her grandson more food. He nodded, too busy eating to reply.

After Haruto had eaten his fill Alfred explained how E-Z's would serve as the team headquarters, or base. He was stalling, searching for the right words to tell them about the danger they'd all be in.

"Let me say, before you agree – that the Furies are evil, horrible creatures who punish children even though they haven't done anything wrong. They've been taking children's lives, for bad thoughts not for bad deeds and hijacking soul catchers from others. We need to stop them and set things right again. And they are extremely dangerous and powerful goddesses."

Haruto's father said, "I forbid you to go!"

"But father, you have taught me that my actions in this life, will carry on into the next. Therefore, I must say yes." He looked at Alfred and said, "Count me in!"

"Haruto, as your mother and father, we want you to succeed – but we want you to be near us, not all the way on the other side of the world with strangers."

Haruto got up from his seat and threw his arms around his grandmother's neck. The two of them whispered back and forth in Japanese so Alfred couldn't understand.

"Sobo says she will accompany me, but she's afraid her time is near. If she dies and isn't in Japan, how will her soul find its way home?"

"We have some archangels and archangel helpers working with us. They are keeping Rosalie's soul safe, and, if anything happened to your grandmother, I'm certain they would protect her soul too. Until their Soul Catchers were ready."

"I'm so proud of you," Sobo said, "and it will be my pleasure to join you on the flight. I'm happy to meet the rest of the superhero children. This Sobo will have more grandchildren." She hugged Haruto.

Haruto's mother and father joined in. It was a family hug. Tears dripped down Alfred's face. A swan crying is the saddest thing on earth.

As they came apart, the dishes were collected and set to wash. Everyone was served tea, except for Haruto.

"I'll get my bag ready," he said. "Goodnight."

"I'll book our flights and let you know the details," Alfred said.

He made his way back to the hotel and booked his flight. Then he sent all the details to Charles Dickens. He hoped Charles could meet them at Heathrow Airport and they'd all fly to E-Z's place together.

After an exhausting day, Alfred jumped onto his Queen Size bed. He mushed the pillows, and watched television until he finally dropped off to sleep.

CHAPTER 7

ON THE WAY

WITH ALL THE CHILDREN on their way to E-Z's house, there was a sense of energy called hope in the air. That energy seemed to spread from one side of the world to the other. So much so, that it reached The Furies.

The three evil goddesses danced around the fire they'd created in a cauldron from the dead bones of the dead. Up rose a multi-headed flaming ball. Right before their eyes, it divided into three fireballs.

The goddesses filled the fireballs with increased energy, until it seemed like the angry spheres would explode. Then they sent them on their way, out to find and crush the hope that lived in the hearts of their enemies.

The first fireball went out, to the farthest destination aligned to meet and destroy E-Z, Lachie, and Baby. The fiery object disintegrated along the way, breaking up from sheer speed, until it was the size of a bowling ball. It zeroed in on the unsuspecting trio it was advancing against.

It was E-Z's wheelchair's sensors which alerted him of the oncoming danger thanks to Hadz and Reiki's upgrade. The GPS detected an inanimate object moving fast, heading right for them.

"Something's coming right at us!" E-Z shouted. "Let's land and get the heck out of its way."

"Righto," Lachie said, as the trio dropped.

But the flaming ball followed them, like it had a tracker of its own. No matter how low they went, it kept on them relentlessly.

They stopped, hovering, grouped together – uncertain whether to land now, or whether to try to outsmart it in another way. If they landed and the thing followed, it could kill or hurt others. They didn't want to put anyone else in danger because it was after them.

"What are we going to do?" Lachie asked.

"You and Baby take cover, let me and my chair handle it."

"We're not leaving you!" Lachie exclaimed and Baby nodded.

"Okay, then get behind me," E-Z said. He knew he and his wheelchair were bulletproof, but were they fireball proofed? He was going to find out, in 5, 4, 3, 2, 1.

Baby extended his neck, let out a roar with his mouth open as wide as it could go – and the fireball went straight into it. The dragon's eyes bulged, and his lips quivered as he contained the fiery beast within. Then off he went, with Lachie holding onto his neck for dear life, flying far and away, searching for a place to relieve himself of the thing which was burning him inside out.

At last, they found the place to drop it safely into the sea. Baby opened his mouth, and out it flew. Still on fire, the thing skidded on top of the water, like it was determined to stay alive but eventually it gave in and fizzled as it sank into the ocean.

"Yes!" E-Z cried. "Way to go Baby!"

Baby and Lachie returned to E-Z's side, "What happened?"

"Baby was amazing! He dropped the fireball into the sea. It's nothing now but another rock."

"Thanks Baby," E-Z said. "That was a little too close for comfort."

"Agreed. And Baby deserves a treat. Something cool for his throat."

"Whatever Baby wants," E-Z said. "Let's go down and have a break before we continue."

Lachie hugged Baby's neck and down they went to shake off their first and they hoped last encounter with a crazy fireball.

"Do you think that was The Furies?" Lachie inquired.

"I don't think they know about us. I mean, they know we exist, but not specifics."

"That thing zeroed in on us. Tried to kill us. Who else would want us dead?"

"You're right, it came straight for us. Probably just a coincidence. I hope."

"Shouldn't we warn the others?"

E-Z looked at his phone. He had zero bars. "My team can handle themselves and I don't want to scare them. Let's hope since it's a one off."

***

THE FURIES SENT A second flaming disc in the direction of Yokohama. Alfred and Haruto's plane was already on the runway preparing to take off.

The fireball flew toward them, but chose an unfortunate route – passing by the 59 ft. robot who reached out its arm, caught it, then crushed it. Ashes burned down on the platform below.

At the airport, Alfred and Haruto's plane took off safely and the pair never knew they were being targeted.

$$* * *$$

T HE THIRD AND FINAL flaming ball went out in the direction of Phoenix, Arizona. It flew around and around, searching for its target for hours but was unable to find it.

Little Dorrit was an exceptional unicorn, with an anti-detection shield at her disposal and it was always at the ready. The protection of her passengers was after all Little Dorrit's key role.

After flying around aimlessly, the flaming ball instead of breaking up with speed, increased in size, until it was the size of a comet. Then it returned home to its rightful owners – The Furies.

The flaming object, which didn't know a friend from a foe, chased the shrieking Furies around Death Valley for hours. They ran for their lives until Tisi conjured a spell.

At first the ball stopped mid-air, and the three goddesses watched it with satisfaction as it dropped into the cauldron and was covered with mushroom stew.

Alli flew toward it, clamping the lid down.

Then The Furies threw their heads back and heckled it, as they danced and sang and laughed.

Until, within the cauldron there was a popping sound. Like kernels of popcorn, heating up. The sounds grew louder, as the lid of the cauldron was dented from the inside, and eventually raised enough so that the newborn fireballs could escape.

The little fireballs, having nowhere to go – zeroed in on The Furies, chasing them about, as one by one they fizzled out.

Singed, exhausted, and annoyed the three goddesses called for Eriel to come and help them, but on this occasion he did not reply.

***

As he flew on across the sky on his own as Lachie and Baby were travelling more slowly due to Baby's side effects from swallowing the fireball, E-Z assessed his team. A couple of times on queue he received texts which confirmed they were thinking about him too.

Lia sent a message, which confirmed Brandy's powers and Alfred had done the same regarding Haruto's abilities.

E-Z hadn't reciprocated by telling them Lachie's powers. Instead, he wanted to go over things to see how he and his team of seven's (including Charles) skills would fare against the three powerful, yet evil goddesses.

Taking inventory in his mind, he reminded himself of his team's assets:

I can fly, so can my chair. We are bullet-proof and I am super strong. I'm a good leader, I'm smart and I have strong empathy.

Lia is inciteful, empathetic, kind, smart, and she can read thoughts and into the future.

Alfred is strong minded, intelligent, and as the oldest member wise with age. He is empathetic, can sometimes read minds, and can heal the sick.

Lachie communicates with creatures. He's a loner, but that's not his fault. He's empathetic, intelligent. He knows how to survive against all odds and he his camouflaging ability will come in handy.

Haruto is the youngest, but he's a survivor. He is able to spin himself invisible.

Brandy has died – several times – and come back to life again. She's a survivor for sure.

Last but not least is Charles Dickens. His abilities are unknown. But he's smart, empathetic and he's able to adaptable.

Using his phone when he had enough bars, he searched historical documents online to find out what abilities The Furies would bring to the table:

Superhuman Strength.

Stamina including high tolerance for pain.

Vitality.

Spider-like agility.

Resistance to injury and superfast healing powers.

Flight.

Shapeshifting – into the form of another person.

Invisibility.

They could inflict pain on their victims.

Meg could secrete parasites. YUCK.

Wait a minute, it says The Furies historically represented justice. It says in the past, they only harmed the wicked and the guilty...that the good and the innocent had nothing to fear. So, what changed? Why did they feel the need to kill innocent children using game play to do it?

He read on, wondering how exactly they were killing the children. According to legend, The Furies never physically harmed any of the wrong doers. Instead, they used guilt – to drive them mad.

He thought back about the boy who'd tried to shoot him. They'd convinced him that if he didn't do what they said, they'd harm his family. He wondered where that kid was now. Was he in one of the Soul Catchers?

He continued searching, to find out if The Furies were capable of mercy and could find no proof of it.

He added to the list something they already knew – The Furies were mortals. That's one thing he and the evil goddesses had in common, and he and his team would need to find a way to use it to their advantage.

Lachie and Baby caught up with E-Z.

"How's Baby doing?" he asked.

"He's doing better now," Lachie replied.

Baby threw back his head, let out a roar and sped ahead.

"Wait for me!" E-Z cried.

CHAPTER 8
THE FURIES

WITH THE FILTHY FEELING of hope still stinking up the air, The Furies waited. They'd repaired their singed clothes and trimmed their burned hair. Luckily, the snakes remained unharmed. To make themselves presentable for their impending guest's arrival.

He was their benefactor. The one who'd brought them back to earth. Suggesting they set up base in the undetectable heart of Death Valley.

Prior to the fireball failure, they'd seen signs. Signs that everything was turning against them now. Change was good, but only if they had control of it. Their time was coming. They had to be ready to move. Things were turning to their advantage. All they had to do was wait for it. Then be ready to pounce.

"Eriel," Meg hissed.

The archangel, their beloved leader had arrived at last.

"What's the latest?" Tisi asked. "We're disgusted with all this hope in the air."

"Yes, this hope stuff is getting us down" Tisi and Allie sang as they danced around the burning fire.

He watched them, dancing naked like banshees. Cracking their whips, while the snakes they had for arms and hair slithered and spit randomly.

Eriel descended upon them like a black cloud, landed, then folded his wings closed. His huge stature made The Furies look like dolls. He stood with his hands on his hips, then went down on one knee to get onto the same level as them. It was his way of lowering himself to their level, while at the same time remaining above them. He wanted them to know they were working for him and not the other way around. He was tired of reinforcing this to the sisters, and yet, it was he feared the only way to keep them in line.

"There is no hope – not now that we're working together," Eriel said. "And don't laugh. Well, I guess you can laugh. It's what I did when I first heard they are sending a team of children to kill you."

The Furies were hysterical. Their voices echoed around Death Valley and scared all the birds away.

"Those idiots!" Meg said.

"We'll eat those children, for breakfast, lunch and dinner," Tisi said, licking her lips.

"We don't eat children," Alli said. "But you are funny, sister. All we want is their souls. And I can't remember WHY we want them. Explain it again dear sister."

Meg said, "We're doing Eriel's bidding. He wants the Soul Catchers and we're getting them for him. Once we fulfil his demands, we'll be Daughters of Nyx – The Kindly Ones - once again and we'll rule the night and do whatever we please."

"Then if I want to taste one of the children – I will be able to, right?" Tisi asked. "I've always wondered what they would taste like." She rolled her eyes and sniffed the air. The snake on her head lunged toward him.

Eriel scoffed. "These aren't ordinary children, like the ones you are stalking in game play. These are gifted children, with powers and abilities. Still, I'll keep you informed, and you'll need my help."

"Your help? To defeat children, mere babies?!" the trio laughed, and they fluttered about lifting off the ground using their powerful batwings. "We'll beat them before they even strike." The snakes hissed and spat in agreement.

"Like we did in the white room. Like we did with their friend Rosalie. She wouldn't tell us who was being sent for us. We wanted to know and were tired of waiting for you to tell us. So, we took her out," Meg said.

"Yes, and you nearly gave the game away! Also, it's a pity you didn't scoop up her soul and put it into a Soul Catcher," Eriel said.

"Now there are loose ends. Loose ends can become leads to those who are searching for them."

They looked up into the sky and saw a streak of colours like a rainbow that stretched from one side to the other. Only it wasn't a rainbow, it was energy. The energy of those whom the archangels had recruited to do what they themselves were unable to do.

"We know they are coming – and they won't stand a chance against us!" Tisi shrieked.

Well, they managed to beat those infantile fireballs you sent!" Eriel exclaimed. "Such a poor and amateurish attempt as it was! It made me ashamed to be working with you! Good thing no one knows about our connection."

With clenched fists and teeth, The Furies did not advance until Alli broke the ice.

"Sisters, his opinion of us doesn't matter. We did our best. It was worth a try. Besides, we already have plenty of souls at our disposal." She stirred the pot, sipping some soup on a ladle, then spitting it out. "Too much salt," she said. She added water, then wild mushrooms, and some baby potatoes. "And we're collecting more children's souls every day. I'm tired of waiting here for the kiddy superheroes to come to us. For them to get organized. When they're all together, why don't we just KILL THEM?"

"Sister, you must be patient."

"I'm tired of being patient. I'm tired of – I'm plain and simple tired," Alli said. She stirred and after tossing in a few wild herbs and spices, she tasted the soup, and it was good. "Supper is ready," she said.

"You will be patient and you will not act – unless I tell you to act. This is my game and I've invited you to play. Without me, you're just three useless goddesses, sleeping the rest of your lives away." He kicked the sand with his boot. "And it's a real pity you must consume human food. Quite a downgrade – since now you require sustenance to survive. When I rule the earth and all the Soul Catchers reside here, I'll hit **EARTH PAUSE.** I will rule the earth and if you play the game right. If you do as I ask you to, then you'll be at my side. Sharing in the winnings. If you go against me, then you will return to dust."

After he spoke the word dust, he opened his arms and wings, lifted off the ground and disappeared.

The Furies sang together while they sipped their soup. The snakes, who were the hungriest, licked it up, and though they'd clean the pot, they still wanted more.

"Now that he's gone," Meg said, "let's talk about our own end game."

Tisi and Alli cackled.

"Eriel believes he will restore us to our Goddess-state, but we're not going to let that archangel take over the earth. Who's to say he won't leave us in the dust when we've done all the work? Archangels don't always keep their promises. We don't need to keep ours either, now do we sisters?"

"Who does he think he is The Chosen One?" Alli asked.

Meg laughed. "He is chosen by nothing and no one – but we still need him."

"Yes," Tisi said. "His self-importance is his flaw." She lowered her voice to a whisper, "Every time he speaks, he weakens himself. Every time he betrays the other archangels, he gives away a little bit more of his power."

Once again the sisters broke into song:

"Blood of recruited children will be tomorrow's soup.

After we sup, we'll have fun with a hula-hoop,"

Meg took up the song,

"Babies, children evil little ones and guilty as muck

We'll say off with their heads if we get all the luck!"

Alli sang,

"Daughters of Darkness vs children who don't have a clue.

The sky will rain down with blood before we're through!"

They cackled and hissed snapping their whips and dancing as the moon rose higher and higher in the sky. Exhausted, they fell to the ground and slept in the dirt. The snakes preferred this position – and slept too – rather than hissing and moving about all night.

"Good night sisters," they said in rounds just like they saw the humans do on The Walton's on television via their satellite dish. It was one of their favourite shows. "And in the morning, we'll revisit the plan."

CHAPTER 9
PAFHS9

IT WAS A COMPETITION for Sam and Samantha who were waiting to see which group of children would arrive back first. The winner would get up with twins every night for an entire month, so stakes were high.

Sam chose E-Z, Lia, then Alfred. Samantha picked Alfred, E-Z, then Lia.

"But E-Z is in Australia," Samantha chided. "You are so going to lose. I'll be thinking of you – NOT – when I'm sleeping the night through for a month."

"You picked Alfred and he's flying on a plane! You know how they always overbook and rarely keep to their schedules. Whereas E-Z can come and go as he pleases and his wheelchair travels amazingly fast! I am so going to win, and I'm so certain, I'll sweeten the bet and make it six months. Are you prepared to increase the bet?"

Samantha considered this new offer. Bets like this could hurt a marriage, and they were already lacking in sleep with both waking up every night to attend to the twins. She hugged him, "Let's just keep it simple. One month."

"Chicken," Sam said, wrapping his arms around his wife. He kissed her on the forehead as Jill let out a wail which Jack soon joined in with. "I'll go," he said.

"Let's go together," Samantha said, taking her husband's hand into hers and off they went down the hall.

Little Dorrit was winging her way back, at top speed.

"Can't we go down and get a drink?" Brandy asked.

"Just no," Little Dorrit said.

"Come on," Lia said, "it'll only take a couple of minutes."

"I don't want to scare you," Little Dorrit said, "but I'm getting a bad feeling and want us out of the open asap."

"Okay," the two girls agreed.

Nearly home now, Lia sent a text to Samantha, telling her they'd be home in a few minutes.

"Ah, we were both wrong!" she said.

"But one of us is still going to have to get up every night with the twins," Sam said.

"We'll take turns," Samantha said, as she and Sam now that the twins had settled back in for their nap, went out into the garden. Soon she could see Little Dorrit, coming in for landing.

Lia and Brandy hopped off.

"That was really cool," Brandy said. "Thanks, Little Dorrit." She hugged the unicorn who replied, "You're welcome."

"Yes, thanks for looking after us," Lia said.

"Looking after you, were there any problems?" Sam asked.

"Nothing I couldn't manage," Little Dorrit said. "Now, if you don't need me for a while, I'd like to get some water and a snack."

"You go ahead," Sam said, "and thanks for looking after our girls."

Little Dorrit winked at Sam, then took off and soon was out of sight.

After the introductions with Sam and Samantha, Brandy called home to let her mother know they'd arrived safely.

A few hours later, Alfred, Charles, Haruto and his grandmother arrived. As before, introductions were made, with Brandy and Lia being added to the mix.

"You can't be THE Charles Dickens," Brandy said, with raised eyebrows. "And you're just a kid, barely out of diapers," she said to Haruto who in response spun himself invisible.

"Oops!" Brandy exclaimed. "And you, you're a big feathery swan! How are you going to help us defeat The Furies!"

"First of all," Alfred began, "you're way more rude than you ought to be. Even an unsophisticated swan like me has manners."

"Anata wa gakidesu!" Haruto's grandmother said which translated means "You're a brat!"

A giggle was heard from invisible Haruto.

Lia stepped in and apologized, "I'll fill her in. She's cool. Just give her a bit of time to settle in," she said. "I didn't know until just now when I saw it for myself what Haruto could do." To the little boy she said, "Come back, Haruto, please. She didn't mean to hurt your feelings."

"Sorry," Brandy said with her eyes lowered to the floor.

Haruto returned, fading in and out. He stood with his arm around his grandmother's waist. Alfred and Charles moved closer to them.

"We just got off a plane and we're tired – so, we're going to go and freshen up. When we return, I expect you'll put a leash on her, or a piece of duct tape over her mouth. Or teach her some manners," he said, then padded off down the hallway with the other two in tow.

"Wow!" Brandy said. "Just WOW! I said I was sorry."

"No, he was right," Lia said.

Samantha said, "You're in our house now, and we won't have you being rude to anyone."

Sam folded his arms across his chest, just as the twins began wailing again.

"They must be hungry. Don't worry I can manage," Samantha said, but before she left, she glared at Brandy.

"Brandy, you're in a strange place, where you don't know anyone other than Lia and Little Dorrit yet," Sam said. "If you want to be a part of this team, to defeat The Furies – then you have to work together. Insulting your teammates isn't an effective way to begin. I'd suggest you apologize again like you mean it when they return, and ask to start again."

Brandy's eyes were filled with tears, "I was just surprised, to see the other team members I'll be working with. But you're right, I will apologize again and ask for another chance. I hope they'll forgive me. Mom always says I'm too outspoken for my own good."

Lia smiled. "You'll love Alfred once you get to know him. This is the first time I've met Charles in person too. Charles is in a strange situation. When he was ten years old, it was in 1822. Think about that. And it's my first-time meeting Haruto and his grandmother too."

"That's crazy! James Monroe was President then – and he was our fifth President!" Brandy hooted. She gently elbowed Lia, "Mom and Dad would be super impressed I remembered that info! And the kid, I mean Haruto, well he seems way too young put his life on the line."

Lia laughed and Sam joined in, then hearing his wife was calling him to help with the twins he rushed out of the room.

Charles replied, "George IV was on the throne when I was here last time. At least I don't have to be worried about going back to the workhouse next year," he said with a smile which faded quickly.

Lia emitted an involuntary shriek, while Brandy burst into tears and said, "I'm so sorry, Charles."

"Ah, so you've heard about workhouses then," he said. "But I'm here and I survived it and apparently went on to use my experience to write about characters like Oliver Twist and Little Dorrit, to mention two. Yes, I've been reading about myself on the internet and have to tell you, I even impressed myself."

"You haven't met Little Dorrit the Unicorn yet," Lia said. "She went off for refreshment, but she'll be back soon."

"Who?" Charles inquired.

On cue Little Dorrit reappeared circling above their heads and came in for a quick landing.

"Little Dorrit, this is Charles Dickens. Charles, this is Little Dorrit," Lia said.

Charles was speechless, as the friendly unicorn nuzzled into him. "I never dreamed in a million years I'd meet a unicorn."

"Pleased to meet you, Charles," Little Dorrit said.

Charles gasped, "And a clever talking one at that!" He had a million questions to ask her, but they'd have to wait because up in the sky, E-Z, Lachie, and Baby were coming in for a landing. "Am I awake or dreaming?" Charles asked. "Pinch me, so I'll be sure."

Once Baby landed and Lachie dismounted, introductions were made all around as E-Z rushed inside to use the bathroom. When he returned Sam and Samantha with the twins in tow, Haruto and Alfred joined them.

"The gang's all here," Alfred said.

"Can I talk to you, and Haruto," Brandy asked. When they nodded, she said, "I'm very, very sorry. Please forgive me for my rudeness and give me a second chance." She looked at her feet.

"Let's do start again," Alfred said.

"Saikai suru," Haruto said then translated, "What he said."

"Anata wa yurusa rete imasu," Haruto's grandmother said which translated means, "You're forgiven."

Baby and Little Dorrit standing side by side was a very strange sight to see. Little Dorrit wasn't little, she was a unicorn which stood over 8 ft. tall, whereas Baby, was no baby in stature, as he was over 18 ft tall.

"Uh, I think you two – referring to Baby and Little Dorrit – are going to need to find somewhere else to sleep as the garden won't be big enough for the two of you," E-Z said.

Little Dorrit said, "I know a place and we can get something delicious to eat and some water too."

"Sounds good to me," Baby said.

Haruto's grandmother patted baby on the head and asked, "Josha wa dodesu ka?" which translated means, "How about a ride?"

Baby said, "Tashika ni, tobinotte!" which translated means, "Sure thing, hop on!"

Haruto ran over and said, "Matte watashi o wasurenaide!" which translated means, "Wait, don't forget me!"

Baby lowered himself down so Haruto and his grandmother could climb up on his back. Off they flew, with Little Dorrit following closely nearby.

Sam said, "I think everyone should get settled in and you can talk and plan to your heart's content tomorrow."

"Good idea," E-Z said, as Baby dropped off Haruto and his grandmother. Sobo's hair was standing on end like she'd put her finger into a socket.

As Haruto's grandmother was speechless, Samantha led her to her room. "Haruto sleeps in my room," she said.

"Sure, I'll be right back." She made her way down the hall to E-Z's room.

"How was it?" E-Z asked Haruto.

"Subarashi!" he exclaimed which translated means, "Fantastic!"

"We had a cot and some bunk beds delivered today," Sam said, "so Haruto, Charles and Lachie, you're with E-Z and Alfred in their room. Alfred sleeps at the end of E-Z's bed."

"Thanks," E-Z said as they headed to his room. "Oh, by the way," he said when they were alone, "did any of you have trouble on the way back?"

Alfred said they hadn't.

"What about you, Lia?" he asked in his mind.

"No."

"So, what happened?" Alfred asked.

"Well, we had a flaming ball of fire on our trail."

Lia gasped.

"But thanks to Baby's quick thinking, it was destroyed."

"How did he manage destroy it?" Alfred inquired.

"Baby swallowed it, then dropped it into the ocean."

"That is scary," Haruto said.

"I'm still a bit worried about Baby," E-Z said, "because on the way back I noticed he coughed and sneezed a couple of times."

Lachie said, "One sparks even flew out of his mouth and nostrils. He says he is fine, but I'm keeping a close watch on him."

"We can't exactly take him to the vet, now, can we?" Alfred said.

Haruto laughed and laughed.

"What's so funny?" E-Z inquired.

"Hyoryu Doragon," he said. "Hyoryu Doragon!" – which translates to dragon veterinarian - and he roared with laughter again.

Alfred and E-Z shrugged their shoulders as did Charles, who changed the subject by asking if the others thought they should come up with a new name for their team since now there are seven of them instead of three.

"Perhaps," E-Z said.

"What are our key characteristics?" Charles asked.

"Promise," Haruto suggested, as he'd calmed himself and had stopped laughing.

"Aspiration," Charles said.

"Faith," E-Z said.

"Hope," Alfred said.

Samantha listened outside the door for a few minutes. All sounded friendly enough, so she returned to speak with Haruto's grandmother.

"Haruto is settling in with the other boys and they are chatting. You can move him in here tomorrow if you want to. He has his own cot in there. They were planning a new name for their superhero team – so I didn't want to break up their brainstorming session."

Haruto's grandmother nodded, "Thank you."

Lia and Brandy were now involved in the room-to-room conversation.

"Strength x 7," the girls suggested.

"Uh, she can sometimes read our thoughts," E-Z confirmed.

Charles exclaimed, "What about PAFHS7?"

"I like it," E-Z said, "but aren't we forgetting two key members of our team? I mean Little Dorrit and Baby. They are integral members and they've saved our butts a couple of times already."

Alfred repeated the words, as did Haruto.

"What about PAFHS9!" Lia and Brandy sang out.

PAFHS9 couldn't help it, they laughed – until they heard someone walking around above their heads on the roof.

"What the heck was that?" E-Z asked.

"Yoo-hoo! It's us!" Raphael said. "Eriel and me.

CHAPTER 10

RUCKUS ON THE ROOF

S AM WONDERED IF CHRISTMAS had come early, when he stumbled outside in his bathrobe to investigate the ruckus on the roof. He couldn't see who was up there, until he was standing in the centre of his front lawn.

"Shhh!" he whispered. "We just got the babies off to sleep."

The archangels didn't reply. Instead, they hung their heads like two scolded children.

"Would you like to come inside?" he asked.

"Thank you, very much," Raphael replied.

POOF

POW

She and Eriel disappeared.

Sam didn't move from the lawn straightaway. His feet were wet from the dew on the grass, and as he jammed his fists into his dressing gown pockets, he spotted Little Dorrit and Baby circling the house.

"Is everything okay down there?" Little Dorrit inquired.

"Yes," Sam said, "but don't go too far just in case. I'll whistle if we need help." He waved, then reentered the house which was now filled with voices and scraping of chairs. He gritted his teeth and hoped the twins were sleeping soundly. Now in the kitchen, he noticed everyone was awake up and about, other than Haruto's grandmother.

Raphael who was seated at the head of the table now resembled the woman who was dressed as a nurse at the hotel when Alfred's life was saved. Her long, flowing graduation like gown increased her status among the others like she was a seated Professor or a Judge.

Eriel, on the other hand, had altered his appearance so he looked like a deceased singer whose trademark was to dress from head to toe in black including dark rimmed sunglasses.

"Do we need more chairs?" Samantha inquired.

"I think we're good," Sam said. "I'm hoping this isn't going to take very long. Oh, and E-Z, you take the other end of the table since you are our elected leader."

"Uh thanks,' E-Z said moving into the position. "So, what the heck are you two doing here in the middle of the night?"

Brandy laughed, "And who said I was the rude one?"

Lia said, "Shhh."

Raphael glanced at each of the children. It was the first time she'd seen Haruto, Charles, Brandy and Lachie. They were all so incredibly young, so brave. Her eyes welled up, as her glance fell upon E-Z. She bowed her head.

E-Z waited, then realized Raphael was asking him to give her permission to speak. He nodded.

Before speaking, Raphael adjusted her new glasses. Her doing so, made E-Z adjust her old glasses which he, as requested by their original owner, never removed from his face.

Charles, who very uncharacteristically was growing more and more impatient asked, "Madam, why am I here as a ten-year-old boy when I'd be far more useful to this team as an adult."

"SILENCE!" Eriel exclaimed, pounding his fists on the table. "We have the floor. Speak, sister, as these children are growing ever impatient. Their eyes are flickering and jetting around the room. As if they expect you to drop them into hot vats of wax!"

"Rude!" Brandy exclaimed. "I'm not afraid of you!"

"Shhh," Lia whispered.

Charles smiled at Brandy.

"You should be afraid," Eriel said with a grimace. "Very afraid."

"Order! Order!" Raphael cried and she waited until all were seated and more calm. "We are here this evening for YOUR benefit." Raphael said rather more loudly than she expected to.

"Here! Here!" Eriel interjected.

"How so?" E-Z inquired.

"She'll tell you if you pipe down!" Eriel stated.

Raphael again waited before she spoke again.

"There is no time for fancy plans or delay. The Furies are wreaking havoc, increasingly every day by pirating Soul Catchers. Flinging old souls out into the open void. It's utter chaos out there! And they are creating more with every second, every minute, every hour of every day. In short, they need to be stopped. Immediately."

"But..." Alfred said, "you didn't even mention the children."

Eriel rose from his chair. He stared at Alfred, forcing him to look away. "She hasn't finished YET."

Raphael continued without hesitating this time.

"We, Eriel and I, are here to give you advice – without being directly involved. Our mission is to help you, to help yourselves to save the children."

E-Z didn't like the sound of this, not at all. He thumped his fists down on the table.

"We have already agreed to battle The Furies. First, we must make ourselves ready, to formulate a plan. When we're ready we will destroy them. If you've come here to rush us, to push us into battle before the time is right, then as I'm elected leader, I'd like to withdraw. We're just kids and you're asking us to put our lives at risk. I'm not, we're not, willing to move forward until we're fully prepared."

Lia stood first and started applauding and the rest of her team joined in.

"What he said," Alfred cooed since swans can't clap.

"Wait!" Raphael said. "We aren't here to push you, we're here to help you."

Eriel's colour changed from white to red, in extreme contrast with his black attire. E-Z and the others looked on, as the archangel's complexion continued to redden, fearful his head might explode.

"Calm yourself and be seated!" Raphael ordered. Eriel took a few deep breaths, then sunk back down into his seat.

Raphael remained calm with her head held high. She pushed her chair back and rose. And kept on rising until she was above the rest. She settled in, like she was riding a magic carpet and tilted her head to the right like she was posing for a selfie.

"We are committed to you and the task, but our powers have limitations. If you're familiar with the saying, 'we're here for you in spirit,' – then that's what we are. We have shredded all the rules today, coming here to your home. We did this against the advice of our superiors and against common sense.

"By coming here, we have exposed ourselves to unseen and unknown dangers, but you're worth the risk. Which is why we decided to come and offer our assistance in person."

"Also, we understand you've been formulating a plan and we're here as your sounding boards. You can test it out on us, see if it flies. If we spot any flaws, we'll point them out and help you."

E-Z glanced at his team members, who sat back down again. "We are considering the option of pulling the goddesses into a game and defeating them there."

"Oh, I see," Raphael said. "You believe you can beat them at their own game, so to speak, clever. Quite clever, but not clever enough I'm afraid."

"What do you mean?"

"They've figured out how to manipulate and control all the players in the gaming world. They know every trick in the book – because the industry has made it easy once you're in the game. To play, you must kill. To advance, you must kill. To win, you must kill.

"Inside the gaming world E-Z, you'll have to kill too. Once you do, you are fair game for The Furies. They could capture each of you, one by one. You can't stand as a team there. Teams within the game are mere illusions. No player would be exempt from their vengeful plot.

"Remember, the goddesses have a mandate – which is to punish the unpunished. And they are following it to a tee, no ifs, ands or buts. However, they are using a grey area to their advantage. Nothing can stop them – provided they keep to the mandate." She stopped and glanced at Eriel, "Anything you want to add?"

"If I were you," he said, "I'd attack them head-on out in the open. Where and when they least expect it. It would put you in a position of power and make them vulnerable."

"That's if they don't see us, or sense we're coming to get them," Brandy said. "I still don't get how they are killing the kids. We must see it, to understand it and to know what we're up against. I said I'd help, but I definitely expected more specific information."

"E-Z," Raphael asked, "are you willing to return my glasses to me? For a short while? With them, I will be able to show you The Furies' technique. How they entrap the children within the game in real time. Brandy is right, seeing is believing, but I can't do it without my original glasses. Only you can make that decision. If you really want to see. If you really want to know."

"Cool," Brandy said. "Let's get to it, E-Z."

Eriel glanced at the ceiling. "Ophaniel has summoned me. I must go now." He bowed.

ZIP

He disappeared into the night.

E-Z took the red glasses off and folded them up, before he handed them Raphael, who was still floating above the table. The glasses, when she reached for them, flew into her hands.

Raphael removed her new glasses and polished the old ones before putting them onto her face. She smiled, as she and everyone else in the room watched the blood move around the frames in its snake-like fashion like it was re-familiarizing itself with her.

When the blood in the glasses had returned to its Raphael flow, she put them on her face then pointed herself toward the wall as powerful bright strobing lights emanated from her glasses, like you'd expect see in a movie theatre.

"Before we begin," Raphael said, "this is not for the faint hearted. What you are about to see is rated Adult Accompaniment. I don't think Haruto should see it."

Samantha said, "Come on Haruto. You and I can watch a little television in the other room."

The two left. And the show began.

On screen was a small boy. Around seven, maybe eight years old. Although it was in the middle of the night, he was sitting in front of the computer. On his head were headphones. In front of his mouth was a tiny microphone which was attached to his headpiece.

"Gotcha!" he said. "At I need is one more kill, then I'll be on the next level."

HHIIIIIIIIISSSSSSSSSSSS.

And they could hear it too.

"You're a murderer!"

"Only bad boys kill – and you're a bad boy. Does your mother know what kind of a bad boy killer you are?"

"I'm playing a game," he said. "It's only a game and if I don't kill, I can't advance."

"Poor kid," E-Z said.

Silence.

The boy resumed his game play. Soon the time came for him to kill again. This time he hesitated.

"Go on. You've killed once, you know it was fun, so go ahead and kill again. You know you want to."

"No!" he said.

"It doesn't matter. One kill is all we need!"

Then the hissing grew very loud again, louder, louder, more loud.

"Stop!" he screamed.

"Stop it Raphael!" Lia screamed.

"I can't," the archangel replied. "You said you want to see how they do it. If any of you are too frightened, leave the room or cover your eyes. Brandy was right, you have to see it for yourselves. Up until now, I haven't seen it either."

HHIIIIIIIIISSSSSSSSSSSS.

Go on. You've killed once, you know it was fun, so go ahead and kill again. You know you want to."

Go on. You've killed once, you know it was fun, so go ahead and kill again. You know you want to."

Go on. You've killed once, you know it was fun, so go ahead and kill again. You know you want to."

"La, la, la, la," the boy sang. Trying to block out the voices.

"He's gone crazy," his friend playing the game too said. "I'm leaving. See you at school tomorrow Tommy."

"La, la, la, la!" Tommy continued to sing.

His pulse raced. His heartbeat sped up. It thumped and pounded, like it wanted to break out of his chest. He couldn't breathe. He tried to stand up, but his legs went to jelly.

He heard a voice in his head. It sounded like his mother's voice, but it wasn't.

"We're so ashamed of you, Tommy. We don't deserve to have a murderer for our son!"

A second voice, which sounded like his father's.

"Our son isn't a murderer, who are you? You're not our son."

Tommy wept.

"I'm a murderer," he said as he slumped down from his chair and crumbled into a ball on the floor.

Now from the screen, two more voices. His brother Alex, his sister Katie, singing a song with his parents, a song which was sung to a popular children's tune about a mulberry bush. Their version went like this:

"Tommy is a mur-der-er; mur-der-er, mur-der-er, mur-der-er, Tommy is a mur-der-er, And we don't love him anymore."

Poor Tommy was all alone now.

"Don't give up," Lia shouted, though she knew he couldn't hear her.

On the floor, rolled up in a ball, he imagined his mother, his father, his sister, and brother were dancing around him. They circled him like a vulture circling her prey.

"Tommy is a mur-der-er; mur-der-er, mur-der-er, mur-der-er, Tommy is a mur-der-er, And we don't love him anymore."

Tommy's little heart was broken. It pushed itself out of his body and flew away.

The Furies caught it, and shoved it into a Soul Catcher. They slammed the door shut.

Raphael removed the glasses. Immediately the wall projector ended. As she handed the glasses back to E-Z, a tear rolled down her cheek.

The silence around the table was deafening.

"They make the witches Shakespeare wrote about in Macbeth look kind," Alfred said.

"I don't see how my power to camouflage, or to talk to animals is going to help, not against them," Lachie said.

"I'd kill one, die, come back, kill the second, die, come back and kill the third," Brandy said. "Let me get my hands on them!"

"Wait a minute," E-Z said. "Now that we've seen it, we need to talk about it. Before plunging in. Maybe we should re-vote? Our participation must be unanimous."

Sam spoke. "You don't have to be ashamed, to say no. No one appointed you as saviors of the world."

"He's right," Raphael said. "No one appointed you – yet there's no one else who can do it."

"Why can't you archangels do it?" Brandy asked.

"We tried everything we knew and failed. That's why we came to you," Raphael said. "And one thing I want to make clear to all of you...If there is ever a moment, when you fear the end is nigh it is then that we will come to help you."

"How do you intend to help us then, when you just told us you're useless?" Charles asked.

"That's what I wanted to ask," Brandy said.

"If, when, the end is near...we archangels will be given other powers. Until they are needed, those powers are asleep deep within the bowels of the earth.

"In the meantime, E-Z, you know the magic words to summon Eriel to your side. Those same words will bring me, and the others should you need us.

"We will come. We will fight alongside of you. But please, do not waste the call. For the ancient powers to awaken, there must be unmistakable evidence that the end of the human race is imminent."

"And what if we call you, and the powers you say you'll have don't come. Then what?" E-Z asked.

"Then we will die alongside of you."

E-Z thumped his fists down on the table.

"Seeing them in action, makes my blood boil. We must defeat them."

"Here! Here!" Charles cried.

"But first," Sam said, "you need to tell these children before you send them in to battle. Tell them exactly how you and the other archangels tried to defeat The Furies."

"We set a trap for them when we discovered they'd come back. It betrayed us, gave us away, and then they moved to Death Valley. Death Valley is out of bounds for archangels now."

"Out of bounds? Who made it so?"

"That is a question I cannot answer. All I know is, a team of immensely powerful archangels were unable to break through the protective barriers they've put into place."

"That's it?" Brandy asked. "That's all you tried, and you want us to take over now. Really."

Raphael put her hands on her hips, "We're archangels and our powers on earth are limited." She laughed, "Our powers elsewhere are limited too."

"Okay, okay," E-Z said. "We get it. We have no choice, not really, but leave it to us."

"Very well," Raphael said. "But before I go, Charles, I wanted to answer your question. The archangels did not summon or release you. We believe your being here, is accidental.

"We don't think The Furies know about you either. Perhaps you are a secret weapon. You may have tremendous powers within you.

"You said, you wished you'd been brought back as a full-grown man. Your age today is significant. We believe children hold the future of the human race in their hands. Only children can defeat pure evil."

"But why only children?" Charles inquired.

"Because they are born pure of heart," Raphael said.

Charles sat a little taller in his seat.

Raphael continued, "Charles Dickens, don't be afraid to experiment and uncover your true self. Within you, there may be a door which only you can open. A key.

"The very fact there is a bloodline, between you, E-Z and Sam, is significant. Don't be afraid, to risk it all to find that key. You're here to help save mankind. There's no doubt about it. Use your time here wisely. Make a difference."

Charles wept as up to this point; he'd felt useless. The others comforted and reassured him.

"Good luck to one and all of you," Raphael said.

POW.

And she was gone.

"When we survive this," Lia said, "and we will survive it, we are going to throw the biggest victory party ever."

"Charles," E-Z said. "If Raphael is right, you could be the most important member of the team. Please take the time to do a little soul searching."

"How does one, soul search?" he inquired.

"Meditation is one way," Brandy said.

"Or walking in nature," Lachie said.

"Alone time, just thinking," Alfred offered.

"Let's get some sleep and continue this discussion in the morning," E-Z said.

"Don't think I'm going to get much sleep after watching poor Tommy," Lia said. "It was even worse than I imagined."

"Yes, poor little Tommy," Alfred agreed.

"So, everyone is still in?" E-Z asked.

"AYEs" were heard from all.

"What about Haruto though?"

"I think he will still be in," E-Z said, "but I'll explain everything to Sobo, and she can talk it over with him. I'd totally understand if they opted out."

"I don't think they will though," Samantha said. "Haruto is sleeping. He felt ashamed because he was too young to see what you were seeing. Like he was less a member of the team."

"You did the right thing, in taking him out of the room," Sam said. "What we witnessed was horrendous."

"I agree," E-Z said.

Charles said, "So, it's all for one and one for all. Just like in The Three Musketeers."

"I always loved that book!" Alfred said.

Even in the direst of situations, books always pulled people together. Each member of PAFHS9 hoped that it was one thing in the world which would never change.

CHAPTER 11
DEJA VU

E-Z AND SAM DIDN'T have much alone time anymore, but neither complained about it. Samantha worried they were losing touch and was determined to set things right by surprising them with an Early Bird Breakfast at Ann's Café.

They arrived in the kitchen at the same time – since they'd both received texts to get dressed and come to the kitchen immediately.

"What's up?" Sam asked.

"Yeah, what's wrong?" E-Z inquired.

"Nothing is wrong," Samantha said. "You two have a reservation at Ann's so head on over there right now – before everyone wakes up and wants to join you."

Sam kissed his wife.

"I thought it was time you too had breakfast together again."

E-Z gave Samantha a big hug.

"We'll make our own way there?"

"Definitely Uncle Sam."

Sam grabbed his backpack with his laptop in it and off they went.

It was a beautiful spring morning with plenty of birdsong to serenade them on the way to the café.

"That wife of yours is pretty special."

"Yes, she's one in a million."

Soon, they arrived at the café. It was nearly empty, and Ann was nowhere to be found but E-Z recognized her sister, Emily. He hadn't seen her since he was a little kid.

"You haven't changed much," Emily said, throwing her arms around him.

"Nor have you," E-Z said, in a muffled voice as she was smothering him in her bulky sweater. "And this is Uncle Sam."

"I can see the resemblance," Emily said, shaking his hand firmly. "I have the perfect table for you, follow me."

When they passed their usual table, he hesitated and glanced at his Uncle. "Mind if we sit at this one instead Emily?"

"Sure thing!" Emily said, laying out the silverware and handing over the menus. "Coffee?" Sam nodded, she poured him a steaming hot mug full.

"Are you having the usual?" she asked E-Z. My sister told me what they might be."

"Definitely."

"And it was a chocolate thick shake, am I right?"

She was spot on.

"And you, Sam?" she asked. "What are you having today?"

"Make that two of what my nephew's having," he said, "but hold the thick shake. Coffee is the only beverage I need this morning."

"Righty-o!" she said, then off she went to the kitchen.

Sam opened his laptop, then closed it again.

"It's nice to come to a place where everything is always the same," E-Z said.

"I should bring Sam and the twins here one day soon. I'd like to support local businesses and it's a good example to set for Jack and Jill."

"Definitely. This place has only good memories for me," E-Z said. "But one of these days I'm going to go out on a limb and order something different. I have to set a good example for my cousins, now don't I?"

Sam laughed, then took a sip of coffee. A second later Emily came by and filled up the cup again. "It's like she has eyes in the back of her head."

E-Z laughed. His mind was hovering around a certain subject he wanted to discuss: The Furies. At the same time, he didn't want to get into the heavy conversation straight away.

"So. My wife is going to have a house full of guests to feed when everyone gets up."

"Sobo will help."

"True, but I don't think we should take advantage. I'd like us to be able to do a replay if you know what I mean?"

"Definitely. So, let's get down to it."

Sam flipped his laptop open again. This time he turned it on and typed into the search engine:

How to defeat The Furies.

E-Z nodded, as his shake was set down in front of him. He immediately tried to sip a bit of his thick shake, but it was too thick to get anything through the straw – which was just the way he liked it. "Anything helpful?"

"It says Erinyes – or The Furies – can only be placated by ritual purification."

"What does that mean?"

"I think it means you would have to perform a deed - at their request, as atonement."

"Doesn't atonement mean the same as penance? I don't like the sound of that," E-Z said. "We haven't done anything to make amends to them for."

"It can also mean Redemption. Repayment. Reparation. Restitution."

"The four Rs, that's catchy but again I ask what we will be repaying them for?

"Think out of the box," Sam said. "What if you could do something, to encourage them to take a hike and leave the children and soul catchers be?"

E-Z laughed. "If there was a way, it would be perfect. Also, too easy."

Sam scratched his head. "Here it says The Furies punished men and women for crimes after death, and during their lifetimes. Which is what they are doing now – kids not adults. I didn't know that."

"What I don't get is, why. Why are they back now? What's changed..."

"All excellent questions which I can't answer," Sam said. "But, oh, here is something interesting. It says as Goddesses of Fate they prevented man from learning about the future."

"How exactly?"

"It doesn't say," Sam said, just as Emily arrived again to refresh his cup of coffee. "Just a little," he said. He was afraid he'd be floating home if he had any more coffee.

"Your breakfast will be up in a second," she said. "Hope you're hungry!"

"We definitely are," E-Z said, as he tried to drink his thick shake again and had some success in getting some up through the straw.

Emily smiled, then went to greet some new customers.

"Before all this," Sam said, "I'd never even heard of The Furies. It says here in both Greek and Roman mythology they were spirits of justice and vengeance. Their other name Erinyes means angry ones." He scrolled down. "I see a few mentions in the gaming world. None of the adjectives used to describe them are contradict what we already know, i.e., The Furies are evil sinister creatures who show no mercy."

"I wish PJ and Arden were back with us. With their game wizarding knowledge, I bet they'd know what to do. Ever since we lost them, I've been kicking myself for losing touch. All because I became too self-involved with being a superhero. I sure do miss those guys."

"They wouldn't want you to kick yourself. And I miss seeing them around too."

Emily put the food down on the table, "Enjoy!" she said.

E-Z and Sam ate greedily, not speaking for a while. After lots of sounds of food enjoyment they resumed their conversation.

"I was just thinking about the plan – to defeat them inside the game. It sure sounded good – or we thought it did until Raphael told us otherwise. It's a good thing she told us straight up though, otherwise...well, I don't even want to think of what might have happened to any of the kids."

"Still, I keep thinking The Furies must have an Achilles heel. Do you remember that story?"

"I do. If they have a weak spot, I don't know what it is. We know they're mortal like us. If they can die, like us, then at least it's a level playing field."

"Let's focus on their weaknesses a little more: anger, grudging, avenging."

"Those are same things they punish others for, so how can it be their weaknesses?" E-Z asked, as he stuffed a forkful of pancakes into his mouth. "So, good."

Sam nodded, "They sure are." He had another sip of coffee. "True, which means we might be able to use the same things they punish others for against them."

"But how?"

"That I do not know – YET."

"We might need more than one of these sessions together to work things through," E-Z said. His second plate full of pancakes was set down on the table in front of him.

"Ann just called and told me to make sure I brought around a second batch of pancakes for you," Emily said.

"Thanks. And tell Ann I hope she's feeling better soon."

"Will do. More coffee?"

Sam nodded, so she refilled his cup. When Emily left, he said, "Uh, be back in a second," and went to the bathroom.

E-Z turned the screen toward him and typed in:

HOW DO I KILL THE FURIES?

Some answers popped up, but they were all to do with how to beat the three goddesses as characters within the gaming world.

Sam returned. "Find anything?"

"Nothing useful. Although it does say The Furies' roots might go all the way back to prehistoric times."

"Well, Baby's lineage also goes quite a way back."

"You should have seen how fast he gobbled up that fireball! Without a second of hesitation."

As they were finished their meal, they thanked Emily and took off home. They were so full they didn't think they'd ever eat again.

"It was sure nice spending the morning with you," E-Z said. "It felt like old times."

"It sure did. Let's do it again soon. In the meantime, let's think more about what we learned today, because as the old saying goes - where there's a will there's a way."

"True, true, Uncle Sam. True true."

CHAPTER 12
BACK AT THE HOUSE

WHEN THEY ARRIVED BACK at the house the first thing Sam did was throw his arms around his wife. She was glad to see him, but her hands were full preparing breakfast.

"Glad you enjoyed it," Samantha squawked.

"Anything I can do to help?" Sam asked, as he assessed the situation with the twins.

"It's all managed," Samantha said, as behind her, the twins let out a wail.

Mostly because Haruto had paused for a moment from playing his version of hon no piku which translated means peekaboo. In Haruto's version, he made a face, then spun really fast until he disappeared, then he'd reappear, and the twins giggled.

"That's very creative!" Sam said, as Lachie stepped in to take over the entertaining role.

Lachie went straight into a few animal imitations and received rave reviews from the twins when he laughed like a kookaburra: **koo-koo-koo-kaa-kaa-KAA!-KAA!-KAA!**

Then it was Charles' turn to entertain with his story called The Three Boulders.

"Iwa?" Haruto said which when translated means boulders.

"Yes," Charles said, as E-Z and Sam retreated to the doorway to listen to the story too, as Alfred, Sobo, Brandy, Lia and Samantha continued with food preparations.

"Once upon a time," Charles began, "there was a hill, high above the English Channel. Upon it were many, many boulders. In fact, too many of them to count.

"On this particular day, a big and heavy truck rolled up the hill, creaking and grinding its gears as it went. When it reached the top, it deployed a boulder lifter, which struggled with the weight of each piece of stone. Over a period of hours, it managed to gather up as many of the rocks as it could. Until the back of the truck was full. Yet not overfull. Overfilling meant boulders would roll off the truck when it moved which was to be avoided at all costs.

"The truck went down the hill. It emptied the boulders into another bigger truck. A truck which was too big to make it up the hill at all, and didn't have a lifting mechanism on it. When the smaller truck was empty again, it went back up the hill. Soon it was full again with boulders.

"This process was completed several times, until the bigger truck was full to the very top. All remaining boulders needed to be transported in the smaller truck. Now that both trucks were full, thc heavy work was finished. So, it was lunch time. And the men ate their sandwiches and drank their thermoses full of hot, sweet tea.

"Back up on the top of the cliff, only three lonely boulders remained. They were sad, having lost their friends and felt rejected, unwanted, unneeded, and quite angry all at the same time. Feeling too many emotions at the same time can be confusing, but sharing feelings with friends, can help, so the three boulders discussed their predicament."

"What are they doing with all our friends?" the first boulder whose name was Rocky asked.

"I don't know," the second boulder whose name was Pebbles said. "Perhaps, they also need friends where they are going. I'll sure miss them."

"No," the third boulder, who was older and wiser and whose name was Craggy said. "They aren't taking them away to see the world. Nor to be their friends. Don't you know that they crush us to make their roads."

"No!" Rocky and Pebbles cried. "They can't pummel our friends into mush!"

"I wish they would have taken me too," Craggy said. "I'm too old to keep sitting up here in all the severe weather. The harsh winds break through my outer layer and I wouldn't mind spending my future as a road. At least then I'd have a purpose."

"A purpose?" Rocky exclaimed. "You call being crushed up and having vehicles run over you every day and every night a purpose?"

"It's better than sitting here, just the three of us forever. I'm tired of the wind and the rain and everything else," Craggy said.

"Well, if you're that keen," Pebbles said, "then all you have to do is roll yourself off the edge. You'd fall right into the back of the truck below and off you'd go with the rest of our friends."

"Oh, it's too far," Rocky said as he rolled himself a bit closer to the edge. "Do you really want to leave us, that much? Can't you find a purpose, by staying here with us? We need you. You're older and wiser."

Craggy moved toward the edge, and peered over the side. It was true, the truck was right there. A few beads of perspiration dripped down. Either they were beads of sweat, or tears.

"It's an awfully long way down," Craggy said. "And it wouldn't be right of me to leave you two youngsters by yourselves."

Pebbles said, "And what if you missed the truck and smashed into bits down there! We'd be up here, with this marvelous view and you'd be down there all alone."

"Besides," Rocky said, "they might come back for us one day. In the meantime, we can chat, and take in the view and the fresh air."

Below them the truck restarted.

CHUGGA CHUGGA VROOM, VROOM.

"It's now or never," Craggy said, as the truck pulled away.

"At least we're together," Rocky said.

"The three boulders crowded together shoulder to shoulder. They turned their backs to the wind, breathed the fresh air and looked out at the beauteous view of the sun setting on the horizon.

"The moral of the story is," Charles began...

Those were the last words E-Z heard before he was back in the blasted silo again.

CHAPTER 13
SILO

"WELCOME BACK!" THE VOICE in the wall said with an exuberance which caused E-Z's shoulders to tense up like someone was standing on them. Reluctant to respond, he rolled his shoulders first forwards, then back, hoping to ease the tension.

"DOT. DOT," a second voice in the wall said, but this time the voice was more quiet, almost a whisper.

He opened his mouth to respond but nothing came to his mind, so he remained quiet, other than the cracking of his fingers which he hoped would ease his tense body.

The first voice, with a more soothing tone asked, "I see you are feeling tense, worried. Is there anything I can get you to pass the time during your wait? A beverage? A book? A journey in your mind?"

She was very perceptive for a voice in the wall, and this helped him to relax a little, however he wasn't keen to take her up on her offer having no idea what a journey in the mind would involve.

"I see you arc hesitant..."

He sat up straight and tall in his chair, and drummed his fingers on the arms like he was rocking out to Deep Purple's Smoke on the Water. He and his father had dueled it on an obsolete version of Guitar Hero, and they'd had a blast. Remembering that moment now, made him feel like his father was in the silo with him.

"Are you sure you don't want a journey in your mind?" the woman in the wall asked again. "You'll have a blast!"

A blast. He'd just used that word in his mind to describe Guitar Hero-ing with his father. No doubt the woman in the wall could read his mind.

"Uh, what exactly is it?" he inquired. "Not saying I want to have a go at it, not until I know more about what it involves."

"Why, it's a place I can send you. A special place where you can live a dream."

It sounded unbelievable...and before he could answer...

DUH DUH DUH,

DUH DUH DUH DUH

DUH DUH DUH

DUH DUH.

He was on the stage, playing lead guitar, with a band he recognized immediately as the original Deep Purple.

The lead singer, who'd left the band but played the original lead guitar on Smoke in the Water didn't seem to mind that E-Z was now playing his part and not doing a bad job of it either. The singer gave him the thumbs up, then walked across the stage to where E-Z was sitting in his wheelchair. Together they played a few riffs as the audience screamed, cheered, and applauded. Next thing he knew he was back in the silo again, but the tense feeling he'd experience previously was now completely gone.

"Thank you! Uh, that was freakin' fantastic! I can't tell you how much it meant to me. I'll never forget it. Ever!" he hesitated and thought the only thing that would have made it better, would have been to have his father up there on the stage with him.

"Sorry I couldn't include your father...but that was only a preview. And you're very welcome. Now, sit tight. Wait time is one minute."

"I think the real thing would blow my mind then!" E-Z said as he leaned his head back and relived the experience again already feeling so completely relaxed, that he could have taken a nap.

PFFT.

The scent this time was different, peppermint and something else he couldn't quite put his finger on.

"It's rosemary," the voice in the wall said.

"Quite refreshing." His eyes were closed, and he was drifting in his mind, when the roof above his head yawned open. He shook his head, opened his eyes, in preparation of what was to come.

Rays of light strobed into the metal container, bouncing, and rebounding from wall to wall. He covered his eyes, to protect them from the unsettling contained light show. When the bouncing illuminations ended, a figure dropped in through the open roof. What an entry she'd made. It was Raphael.

"Uh, hello," he said. "That was quite an entry."

"I've been promoted," the archangel admitted, "and a certain amount of flourish is required. Perhaps, a little over the top in this case, but it's a relatively new promotion. All promotions have a learning curve."

"Congrats on the promotion."

"Thank you, now let's get down to the business of why you're here."

"Sure thing."

E-Z waited patiently for Raphael to speak again, but for some time she did not. Instead, she flitted about, like a bird testing its wings for the first time. Was she showing off? If yes, why? Then he saw it, she was wearing a brand-new pair of eyeglasses. These were bigger, more distinctive looking with larger frames and thicker lenses and made her look like a female version of Mr. McGoo.

"Uh, nice glasses," he lied.

"They weren't my first choice," Raphael admitted, "but they'll have to do." She moved closer to where he was seated and hovered. "It seems." She stopped and moved about uncomfortably.

SKIDOO

A chair arrived, which she sat in for a second.

SKIDOO

And it was gone. She hovered again. Placed her open palm on the side of her face. "A few things have been brought to our attention. I don't mean that in the royal sense, I mean it as in all archangels."

"Such as?"

Again, she fidgeted.

"Should I ask the wall to spray some lavender to relax you? You seem rather tense."

Then she was in his face screeching, "LAVENDER DOESN'T WORK ON ARCHANGELS! It's a vile, human..." She took a deep breath. "I'm very sorry."

"It's okay. I get it, you have bad news to tell me. It's better to rip the band aid off. What I mean it, just tell me straight up."

"Very well. Here goes."

E-Z leaned closer, "Okay, shoot."

From the speakers in the wall a song played, something about shooting a sheriff.

He hummed along at first, "Stop!" E-Z commanded. "And tell me why I'm here."

"He wants to get right down to business," Raphael said to herself. "Well then, here it is. I'll get straight to the point."

"Okay you do that." E-Z said, wishing she would.

"In a nutshell," she said, "Eriel has been caught red handed – playing for both sides."

"Playing what?" Then something in his mind tweaked. "No, you can't mean that he betrayed us?"

She tapped her bony finger on her chin, while E-Z opened and closed his mouth like a minnow out of water.

"Yes. Eriel was personally responsible for your friend Rosalie's demise. He also was responsible for the destruction of The White Room. All him. All Eriel."

E-Z took it all in. Poor Rosalie. "Wait! Wasn't he working for you? I mean, weren't you in charge of him? How could this have happened on your watch? I've read some things about archangels, but betraying kids who are volunteering to help you is as low as you can go. I guess leopards don't change their spots."

"I wasn't in charge of Eriel. He and I were co-workers, comrades. We worked together and I thought respected each other. I was wrong."

"And yet, you were promoted."

"I was, but the two things weren't directly connected. All I can tell you is, Eriel was once one of us, now he's not. After betraying us, and you. After turning his back on his principles – everything we stand for – he's out. I mean permanently out."

E-Z gasped. "Are you telling me, that Eriel has exposed us? By us, I mean me and my team?"

"Michael, who is our leader, has been questioning Eriel. It took some doing to get him to talk. But he has confessed to bringing The Furies back to earth. To using them to advance his station. There's no redemption. No forgiveness for Eriel."

"I'm speechless. How did this happen?"

"How? Well, if we knew how then we'd know why – which we don't. What we do know is he's Eriel and Eriel always does what is best for Eriel. We knew he had issues, and yet, we kept giving him opportunities to prove himself – and when he failed us – we forgave him and gave him another chance and another chance. We kept believing in him until now. He is finished. Done."

"Done? You mean dead? Do archangels die? And why did you give him so many chances? Don't you know the saying, three strikes and you're out?"

"Yes, I've heard that baseball terminology, but we're archangels and we are all expected to fail, or to relapse on some level. And you're right about the Garden of Eden incident. Our history goes way back...but we thought we were doing better, improving. I myself am the Patron Saint of young people, like you and your friends.

"That's why I suggested we work with you to defeat those horrible Furies. Why, it was Eriel who encouraged me to do so. He's the one who discovered you. Who sent Hadz and Reiki to you. Up until those horrible sisters arrived, we were adding something positive to all of your lives...We were giving you purpose. Remember the times when you wanted to give up? You didn't because we helped you to keep going."

"Okay, I understand Eriel is a baddie. What does this mean for me and my team? From where I'm sitting, our mission has been compromised. So, we're out and I think you ought to move on to Plan B."

"Problem is," Raphael said, then stopped, as the ceiling above reopened and Ophaniel arrived without any flourish at all as she floated down toward them.

"Long time no see," Ophaniel said directed at E-Z. Then to Raphael, "Is he up to speed?"

"Yes, he is. And I'm sure glad you're here because he wants to know what our Plan B is."

Ophaniel nodded. "Very well. To put it as clear as it can be, we don't have a Plan B or C or D – because you and your team were all our Plans rolled into one."

E-Z shook his head in disbelief. "Haven't you archangels heard the phrase, don't put all your eggs into one basket?"

Ophaniel laughed. "Yes, its origin is from Cervantes' character Don Quixote, but it never really made sense to me. Possibly because we archangels don't eat eggs. The mere thought of their jelly-like yokeiness – yuck - makes me want to hurl."

"Me too," Raphael said, covering her mouth with the back of her hand. "Besides their disgusting appearance, why would one put eggs into a basket at all? Why not a bowl? If you are preparing eggs..."

"Agreed," Ophaniel said. "I've seen Jamie Oliver cook an omelet. He uses a bowl first, then he cooks them."

"Oh, brother and I can't believe you archangels watch any television let alone Jamie Oliver." He shook his head. "It means if you put all the eggs together, in one place – like a basket or a bowl or pan or whatever you prefer – if you drop the basket or bowl or pan – then all the eggs will be broken and spoiled by the shells – so you'll have no eggs for breakfast."

"But don't chickens lay eggs every day? So, if you don't get eggs today, you just come back tomorrow," Ophaniel said.

"What's one day without an egg?" Raphael inquired.

E-Z opened his hand and slapped it against his head. "Argghh!" The archangels looked at him and waited while he breathed in very deeply then exhaled very loudly. "What are we going to do about this Eriel situation?"

"First," Ophaniel said, "here returning to you today, by your special request are, drumroll - your two friends..."

POP

POP

Hadz and Reiki, or what resembled the two wannabe angels arrived. They were blackened with soot, from head to toe. Their petals were wonky, torn, some were open and up, some were dead and withered. Their wings drooped, like they'd forgotten how to fly or had no will to anymore, and their faces, the expression on their faces was one of extreme despair.

"Wh-what happened to them?" he asked.

Ophaniel moved nearer to the two displaced wannabe angels and they recoiled.

"You're safe now," Raphael said, in a soft motherly voice, which caused them to break into sobs, which turned into wails.

Ophaniel covered her ears, then moved nearer to E-Z and whispered. "Eriel had them imprisoned. It took us some time to find them this time. Poor things couldn't help themselves because he stripped them of their powers."

"Poor things," E-Z said.

E-Z, Ophaniel and Raphael turned toward the creatures. Hadz and Reiki attempted to smile. They didn't even come close.

The two thrashed about, like they were fending off a pack of vultures.

"Be still," Ophaniel said.

Hadz and Reiki ceased movement. Now they sat like a pair of dirty dolls with their eyes fixated at nothing and no one. They were a shadow of their former selves.

"I don't mean to be rude," E-Z whispered, "but in their current state, they aren't going to much help to us. That's if you can convince us to go ahead with this plan under the circumstances."

E-Z's words hit the two wannabe angels like a slap on their face.

POP

POP

"How very rude and unnecessary cruelty!" Ophaniel scolded before she disappeared.

ZAP

"You've shown us a very cruel side of your character E-Z Dickens and if your mother and father were here, they'd be ashamed of you."

"Sorry," E-Z said, "but don't you ever talk to me about my parents. To you archangels, they are off bounds. Got it?"

Raphael nodded.

"Besides, I didn't mean to hurt their feelings. Of course, we can use them. If we have to fight The Furies, then we're going to need all the help we can get. Come back please Hadz and Reiki. Give me another chance."

Nothing.

E-Z tried again. "Come back and you will be very welcome members of our team."

POP

POP

The pair were now clean and tidy like their old selves.

"Welcome back," E-Z said.

Hadz and Reiki flew over to him. Each took a place on one of his shoulders. They trembled, involuntarily, frightened of their own shadows.

"It'll be okay," he said. "We'll have your backs now you're a member of our team."

They tried to smile, and he appreciated the effort.

"So," E-Z said, "what exactly did Eriel tell The Furies about us?"

"He told them we were sending kids to defeat them – that's all."

"That's what he told you? How do we know he isn't lying? And how do we find out what The Furies' endgame is?"

"We think we know that The Furies and Eriel's end game was to control the earth. They were going to hit EARTH PAUSE and turn it into New Hades, i.e., hell on earth. Where they could rule, by forming a team of souls who'd be at their mercy. Yes, they'd let souls out to roam freely, but once they had their freedom – they'd have to give it up."

"Why would they agree to give it up?" he asked.

"Because humans, even human souls cannot process the concept of freedom. Instead, they prefer to be constrained. Lack of freedom is the human security blanket."

"That's a lie," E-Z said. "Makes me so angry! We humans can appreciate our freedom. We love nature, being able to breathe in the air, to share our thoughts and feelings with others, to appreciate the world and all we have in it."

"Angry enough to fight for your freedom and for the freedom of others?" Ophaniel said.

E-Z hadn't even noticed she'd returned.

"Yes," he said. "but tell me, in this new world of theirs, they'd only choose the souls who they could control. What would happen to the others?"

"They'd float around forever, with no homes," Raphael said. "In this new world of theirs, the afterlife would be eliminated. The earth would forever be in the state of pause. Souls would remain in bodies which no longer were alive, nor would they be dead. No more hearts would beat. No more love or children to be born. No souls to ascend – anymore – ever."

E-Z remained quiet, thinking, taking it all in.

The voice in the wall asked, "Would anyone like a refreshment?"

"No thank you," he said, but he was happy for the interruption as it brought him back to the moment. "I understand what Eriel was using The Furies to do. The fact remains that he is an archangel like you, and you knew he had issues, still you gave him chance after chance even when he didn't deserve it. So, now I'm wondering why we, myself and my team should fix what one of your own archangels has screwed up?"

"Because..." Raphael began.

"I wasn't finished yet," E-Z said, "before when you and Eriel visited my house, when he met my family, and the other team members, we thought he was on our side. He's seen where we live. He knows all about us. We're in grave danger because of him."

"This is true," Ophaniel said.

"Undeniable and we are very sorry," Raphael said.

"Have Eriel call them off. He created this mess, and he should fix it." He crashed his closed fists down on the arms of his chair causing Hadz and Reiki to jump and shiver. He patted the wannabe angels on the head. "It's okay, I'm sorry to upset you."

"Bravo!" Hadz cheered.

"Hurrah!" Reiki called out.

Raphael and Ophaniel said in unison, "Eriel is constrained deep within the bowels of the earth. He's in a place where no human should dare to go. In short, he cannot be reached."

"But we escaped from the mines, once," Reiki said.

"Twice," Hadz said.

"He's not in the mines, he's in another place, further down, not as far down as in the fires, but in another place where it is so cold that everything turns to ice, even blood flowing through veins. A place where no human could survive!

"Eriel is also powerless there since his have been stripped away. He is under lock and key, he sees no one. Hears nothing. He will never be allowed out of that place – EVER."

"I want to speak to him," E-Z said. "I need to ask him questions – questions only he can answer."

Raphael and Ophaniel shouted, "You cannot! You must not!"

"Then I withdraw my team's support. Please return me to my home. Haruto and the others can return to their families." He stopped speaking as a flash of PJ and Arden flashed in his mind. If he didn't do anything, they'd be stuck in comas, maybe forever.

He remembered all the times they'd helped him. His first day back at school in a wheelchair. The time they reintroduced him to playing baseball – had all the guys on the team on the field to greet him. The time they helped him through it all when his parents died. A tear fell down his cheek. He wiped it away.

"TAKE HIM!" a voice in the wall thundered.

Then it suddenly became very, very cold. So cold that imagined he could really feel the blood in his veins turning to ice.

CHAPTER 14

ERIEL ON ICE

ALL ALONE. SO VERY all alone. And so cold, so very very cold. It was like he was inside a hollowed-out ice cube. When he breathed in, the ice filled his lungs.

He went to the edge. He breathed into it. It fogged up. It wasn't an ice cube; it was a glass cube. And there was a handle. It looked like it was made of medal. Fearing his skin would stick to it, he used his shirt and opened it.

What was inside, was a collection of warm blankets, duvets, cardigans, hats, gloves – the lot. He reached in and layered up.

As he put his arms into the cardigan, his mind flew back to a time when his father wore a similar sweater on a skiing trip. It was green, like this one was, and on the outside, it felt scratchy to touch but, on the inside, it was as warm as toast. As he pulled it around him and buttoned the front, the oaky smell of his father's favourite shaving lotion filled his nostrils. smelled his father's shaving lotion in it. A strong feeling of déjà vu overpowered him, when he put his fingers into a pair of black velvet gloves – gloves which he swore had belonged to his father. They couldn't be though since everything was destroyed in the fire. He wrapped his arms around himself, trying to get warm. Figuring it was cold taking over his body and mind.

He pushed away some other items, discovering a blanket at the bottom of the box which he recognized immediately. Hand knitted, by his mother on the sofa night after night and when it was completed it took its place – on the back of the leather sofa. For the movie nights and to cover his eyes if something scary happened.

He removed the gloves and touched it, to see if it was real and then brushed it against his cheek. The flowery scent of his mother's perfume reached him, comforted him. A tear ran down his cheek, as he reapplied the gloves, then wrapped his mother's blanket around his father's cardigan. He wore the blanket like a hood, and took in his surroundings.

Over his head, but pointing down with their sharp spikes were stalactites made of ice in all sizes and shapes. If one of them dropped, they'd pierce the top of his skull and carry on through him all the way to his toes. He wished he had a construction hat -

BINGO

And a yellow hard hat appeared on his head, then another and another and another. He felt like Curious George, and smiled. Now he was ready for anything.

He searched for a door, inching his way along the walls of the cube. No handle was visible. What kind of prison had they dropped him into?

At last, he found edges, in the centre of the right wall. He removed a glove and used his fingernail to scratch the surface of what he soon discovered to be a window. What he saw, did not make him feel less anxious. His cube was one of many stretching along the tunnel as far as the eye could see. No occupants were visible behind their own cubicles glassed-over windows.

He breathed on the glass and wrote in the word, "HELP!" spelled backwards in case anyone saw it. Then he quickly erased it remembering who he'd come to see: Eriel.

E-Z moved along the front of the cube, to the far side and once again he found a frame which he was certain was a window. He scraped the surface away and soon found who he was looking for: the traitor.

The once powerful archangel looked pathetic, like someone had pricked him with a pin and let all the air out. His body was fastened to the wall. At first, E-Z thought he was being held in place by gravity or some kind of an invisible force, but then he realized upon closer inspection that Eriel's entire body was contained within a thick block of ice. Eriel's cube had been molded to his body, therefore ice water filled every nook and cranny of his form and he, unlike E-Z did not have access to blankets.

CLANK. CLANK. CLANK.

E-Z craned his neck to the left when he heard the sound of footsteps reverberating. He could feel the thing was getting closer, but he couldn't see it.

CLANK. CLANK. CLANK.

E-Z shook his head. He had to focus, to stay in the moment, and yet, he was experiencing another strange feeling of déjà vu.

His mind flew back to the dream, he had some time ago about a birthday party with PJ and Arden. In that dream, a hooded figure had arrived, making a similar sound. The dream had been about finding a missing baseball cap.

As the sound became deafening, he caught a glimpse of the figure, who was a warrior, larger than life with wings the size of two full grown maple trees. In one hand, the archangel carried a golden shield and in the other a sword. E-Z shielded his eyes as the light hit the hull of the sword.

CLANK. CLANK. CLANK.

The archangel warrior stopped in front of Eriel, who did not raise his eyes to meet the newcomer's gaze.

Until he stopped, E-Z hadn't noticed the archangel's huge wings, which while he had been walking, had been at rest. Now, the warrior raised himself up, so that his and Eriel's faces were level.

"You have a visitor," he said.

Eriel's eyes remained lowered.

"Your eyes do not fool me," the warrior said. "You've shamed yourself. You've shamed us all – and yet, you do not feel sorry, and you do not repent. Speak to me. Tell me why I should allow you to have a visitor at all."

Eriel continued looking at floor, as he mumbled something inaudible.

"Speak up!" the warrior demanded.

"I do repent!" Eriel spewed. "I repent having failed to…"

"Silence!" the warrior demanded.

CLANK. CLANK. CLANK.

Now the warrior was standing on the other side of the glass, face to face with E-Z.

"I am Michael," he said.

"Uh, hi, I'm E-Z." He knew the man's voice. He was the one who ordered Raphael and Ophaniel to let him speak with Eriel.

"Arise," Michael said.

"I can't walk," he said.

"You can if I say so," Michael revealed, "and I say so. Arise E-Z Dickens!"

E-Z felt like one of those preparing to be healed at a service on television. Reluctantly, he lifted himself out of his chair. He legs wobbled a bit, mostly from fear than disbelief. After all Michael was the most powerful archangel. Seconds later, E-Z was standing tall inside the ice wall.

"You asked to speak with, that thing, that fallen thing over there on the wall. He will not help you as he is rotten to the core. And yet he SHOULD help you. He SHOULD help all of us in order to save himself from turning into an ice sculpture – a permanent fixture of this place."

With every word spoken, Michael's voice made E-Z feel stronger, and more confident.

Eriel raised his eyes.

For a second E-Z glimpsed something there. Was it defeat? Was it remorse?

Eriel closed his eyes as his body went limp within the ice prison which was holding him.

"I think he fainted," E-Z said.

CLANK. CLANK. CLANK.

Michael returned to have a closer look at his prison of ice. A serpent slid out of the top of his boot, and began crawling toward the face of Eriel. The thing slithered its way up, up, with its forked tongue moving back and forth like it was hungry for blood.

Michael said, "My friend's body is melting his way toward your face Eriel. Aren't you going to open your eyes and say hello?"

Eriel did open his eyes, and seeing the snake making its way up his body, he let out a scream.

"GARUUUUUUUUUUUMMMMMMM!"

Michael snapped his fingers and the snake ceased movement. Using his fingernail, Michael scraped the ice. Within it, Eriel's body vibrated. Like he was being electrocuted.

"MMMMM,hhhhh,MMMMMMM!"

"Stop!" E-Z cried covering his ears. "Please!"

Michael ceased scarping. He raised his arm, and the snake wound itself around and slithered its way back to inside his boot.

"This boy shows you mercy Eriel. It is more than you deserve."

Eriel continued moaning in despair.

Michael continued, turning toward E-Z, "I will give you five minutes to ask Eriel any questions you may have."

Then to Eriel, "We can compel you to speak to him, but I would prefer it, if you chose to help him of your own volition. Once upon a time you chose to save this young boy's life. He in turn repaid his debt. Now, you've betrayed us and you have to re-earn our trust."

Michael raised his foot and kicked the ice structure in which Eriel was encased. It shook, but did not crack or shatter.

"You disgust me! You expect this human boy to fix your mistakes. To in fact right your wrongs. Still, he wants to give you a chance to answer his questions. So, help him. This is your only chance, your only opportunity to prove to us that you still have something within in you worth saving. Some part of you that has not yet turned rotten to your core."

Eriel raised his eyes, "Sire." He lowered them again.

"You may be forgiven, but if you choose not to help him – your lack of cooperation will be duly noted."

Eriel's eyes remained focused on the floor.

"Do you understand?" Michael asked. When Eriel did not respond, Michael's voice thundered forth with, "DO YOU UNDERSTAND?"

It seemed to E-Z that the ice all around him shook and trembled at the very sound of Michael's voice and he was grateful once again for all the helmets protecting his skull. He hoped they would be enough, otherwise he'd be buried in this place with Eriel and Michael forever and he'd never see Uncle Sam, or his friends, ever again.

Eriel nodded.

"Five minutes," Michael said.

CLANK. CLANK. CLANK.

And he was gone.

He and Eriel were alone.

E-Z moved closer to Eriel and asked, "How can we beat The Furies?"

Eriel opened his mouth to speak, but said nothing. He closed his eyes.

"Please," E-Z pleaded. "Please help us."

CLANK. CLANK. CLANK.

Michael was back already. It couldn't have been five minutes – not yet. He'd learned nothing, nothing at all from Eriel.

Eriel with his teeth clenched and chattering whispered three words: "Use Raphael's glasses."

"What?" E-Z yelled, pounding his fists against the ice wall. "How?"

The next thing he knew, he was back in the kitchen doorway again. He was no longer wearing his parents' garments, but the combined scents of his father's shaving lotion and his mother's perfume lingered. He hugged himself and listened as Charles explained the moral of his story.

"The moral of my story," Charles said, "is, everything is better when you have friends to share it with."

"Oh," E-Z said, as Samantha announced breakfast was served.

"Line up here. Grab a plate, napkin, and cutlery. Help yourself," she said. "It's a smorgasbord."

Sobo said, "Sumogasubodo!" to Haruto who squealed in delight.

"I made some sushi," Samantha said. "It was my first time."

Sobo nodded, "Thank you, but next time let me help you."

Samantha nodded, "That would be wonderful."

E-Z moved his chair forward.

Uncle Sam whispered walking alongside of him, "Where did you go? I mean you were there, and your chair was there, but you were somewhere else too, weren't you?"

"Uh, yes, I'll explain later. I need time to process everything that happened. Give me a few minutes. Oh, and by the way, thanks."

"For what?" Sam asked.

"For breakfast, it was like old times. Fun."

"Let's make sure we do it again soon."

"Definitely," he said as he made his way to his room.

CHAPTER 15
HOME SWEET HOME

NOW ALL ALONE, IT felt good to know that Eriel was no longer a physical threat to them. He'd been incapacitated thanks to Michael, but only after he'd betrayed everyone.

Eriel had gone way too far, but why? Why would he betray his own kind? Knowing full well Michael was more powerful than him. It made no sense.

POP.

POP.

"Welcome home!" he said.

Hadz and Reiki landed in front of him on the bed, "Thank you, E-Z. You always treat us kindly."

"I'm sorry Eriel was so terrible to you. It's good he's locked up now. It's what he deserves."

"What did you think of them?" Hadz asked.

"Not sure what you mean."

"We sent the crate."

"Oh, maybe it didn't work," Reiki said.

"That was you?" E-Z's eyes teared up.

"Glad it arrived safely," Hadz said as the pair of wannabe angels' smiles stretched across their faces in such a way that it seemed the rest of their features were diminished.

"Thank you so much. I thought everything belonging to my parents had been destroyed in the fire." He took a deep breath fighting back the tears. "I only wish, I could have brought it back here with me. Although it meant a lot, to even just have it for..."

ZAP.

"All you had to do was say the word. They are yours, after all," they said.

It was there, at the end of his bed. His parents' crate, or what they called their blanket box. In it were treasures he'd gone through as a kid. And now it was his. A tangible treasure chest filled with memories of his parents.

"But how?" he asked.

"We managed to save a few things, by popping in and out when the house was burning," Hadz said.

"We decided to keep them safe for you, until you were ready to have them back. We hope the timing was right."

He moved, like in a dream toward the chest and opened the lid. A waft of his father's musky-woody after shave blended with his mother's sweet-citrony perfume greeted him like an embrace. Careful not to let it all escape at one time, he gently closed the lid.

"I can't thank you two enough. I'll never be able to thank you. I'll go through everything, another time. Again, thank you both so very much." He held out his arms and the two wannabe angels flew into them.

"He's getting too soppy," Hadz said.

"Anyone tell you; you need a haircut?" Reiki asked.

E-Z finger combed his hair and patted down the centre part which, due to being in the freezing cold bowels of the earth was standing up like bristles in a brush. "Better?"

"A little," Hadz said.

"Okay, I need to focus. The others will be in here soon for an update on the Eriel situation. I need to tell them about Michael. Think they'll be impressed I met him?"

"It doesn't matter if they're impressed," Hadz said. "What matters is, did Eriel tell you anything worthwhile?"

"Yes, but I'm still trying to figure out what he meant."

"Tell us, maybe we can solve the mystery!"

"What who meant?" Alfred asked, as he poked his beak into the room.

"Come on in," E-Z said.

Alfred waddled in. It was molting season and a few feathers fluttered behind him. "Hello Hadz, hello Reiki."

"Hi," they replied.

"Long story, but to get straight to the point I was summoned back to the silo where Raphael and Ophaniel filled me in on a situation about Eriel. He's been working on all sides. Pretending to be allied with us, the archangels and The Furies. Don't worry, his betrayal was discovered and he was captured and imprisoned. He is under guard by the head archangel Michael who let me speak with Eriel briefly."

"And what did Eriel say?" Alfred inquired.

"I only had time to ask him one question. So, I asked him how we could beat The Furies. That's why I came in here, to think about what he said."

"Ah, so you wanted to be alone?" Alfred asked. "Come on Hadz and Reiki, let's give E- some peace and quiet." He moved toward the door, but they remained where they were.

"A problem solved is a problem shared," they sang.

"True. And it was the moral of Charles' story."

"Alright, gather round." He paused, then said, "Eriel said we should use Raphael's glasses."

"Right, that's it?" Alfred said. "I can see why you're not sure what he meant. It's very vague."

"I know. And he didn't say how to use them."

Hadz leaned over and whispered something to Reiki.

POP.

POP

And they were gone.

"Perhaps, begin from the beginning. Tell me exactly what Eriel told you."

"I already did. He said use Raphael's glasses. That was it. Michael had us on a time clock. At first, I thought Eriel wasn't going to say a word. He said those three word and the time ran out. Next thing I knew I was back here again."

Alfred paced, and noticed the blanket box at the end of the bed. "What's this then?"

"It belonged to my parents," E-Z said fighting back the sobs. "Hadz and Reiki rescued it from the fire. They just told me they rescued it for me – put their lives at risk even."

"That was so," he teared up, "thoughtful of them. Have you been through it yet?"

"No, but I will."

"What was Michael like?"

"He clanked a lot when he walked. It reminded me of the dream I had about PJ, Arden, and the guillotine."

"Oh, I remember you telling us about that dream. Was he as scary as the executioner?"

"Michael was very cross and rightly so. Eriel betrayed him, all the archangels and us. What I don't get was what could be worth such a risk?"

"Power – some people would do anything to get it. But what we need to figure out, how we can use Raphael's glasses to stop the plan Eriel and The Furies put into motion."

E-Z removed them from his face. When he wore them, the blood didn't pulse and move around in the frames, like it did when Raphael wore them. On him, they were just like any other eyeglasses.

"Command the glasses to do something," Alfred suggested.

"Glasses disappear," E-Z commanded.

He dropped them and they landed on the floor.

E-Z sighed. Two heads definitely weren't better than one in this case. He laughed.

"It was good to see Hadz and Reiki back. Are they here to stay? I mean, to help us?"

"They are, but they've been through a lot lately and they might be suffering from PTSD – that's post-traumatic stress disorder."

"Yes, I know. What happened?"

"Eriel happened, that's what. He's been wreaking chaos and havoc on earth and everywhere else from the sound of it." E-Z paused. "What if I used the glasses to change my form?"

"And do what?"

"If I could change my form, I could visit The Furies as Eriel."

"That would only work, if they weren't aware, he'd been caught," Alfred said.

"Yeah, but if they didn't know. Think of the damage I could do. I could go in there. They'd think I was on their side. And I could turn on them. BAM I could knock them right out of the park!"

POP.

POP.

"It would be way too dangerous!" Hadz shrieked.

"Wayyyyyyyyyyyyyy toooooooooooo dangerous!" Reiki echoed.

"Besides, we have another idea."

"Tell us," E-Z said.

"They've recreated The White Room, so we went back there to see if there are any books about Raphael's glasses."

"And? Was there a book?"

"No," Hadz said.

"But we did find this," Reiki said.

It was a tiny booklet, around the size of the end of E-Z's index finger. The title on the spine read: *Raphael's First Book of Enoch*.

Hadz and Reiki flipped through the pages since the book was the perfect size for the two of them to hold together.

"It says here," Hadz read aloud, "Raphael's purpose was to heal the earth which the fallen angels had defiled."

"Remember, Raphael said, I can only call upon her when the end is nigh? Perhaps, the glasses will only reveal their powers to me when they're needed too."

"Exactly," Hadz and Reiki agreed.

"I think we need a brainstorming session with the others, but your idea to change your appearance to Eriel's is a good one," Alfred said. "We'd just need to figure out how to back you up when you were doing it – to keep you safe."

"That's a bad idea," Hadz said.

"A very bad idea!" Reiki said.

"How so?" Alfred inquired.

"First, you don't know what The Furies know."

"Or do not know."

"Second, it could be a trap."

"A trap orchestrated by Eriel and The Furies."

"Third, and most important of all,"

"Eriel is terrified of Michael."

In unison they said, "Raphael's glasses must hold the key to everything. Eriel is seeking forgiveness and redemption by Michael and the other archangels. It's his only hope. You are his only hope. Therefore, we believe he told you the truth."

"But what if The Furies don't know about Eriel's – situation? While they are in the dark, we have an advantage here," Alfred said.

"I agree," E-Z said.

Lia stuck her head in the room, followed by the rest of the gang. "What's up?" she asked.

"Come on in and I'll explain. Oh, and close the door behind you."

"Sounds dubious," Lia said. She noticed Hadz and Reiki and waved to them. Then she closed the door behind them and locked it.

CHAPTER 16
WHAT TO DO

"TAKE A SEAT, GET comfortable," he said, as everyone piled onto his bed. "First, to those who haven't met them yet - this is Hadz, and this is Reiki. They are friends and wannabe angels. They've been appointed to help us."

Haruto bowed, Lachie said, "Good 'day!" Charles and Brandy shook hands with them.

After everyone was formally introduced, the team sat along the side of the bed. E-Z thought they looked like passengers waiting for a bus.

"We're all here, to defeat The Furies. But there's some current information we need to consider. Before we move ahead."

"What do you mean?" Lia asked. "Are you suggesting we might opt out?"

E-Z cleared his throat.

"It's best if you let me tell you everything, then you can ask questions. I probably should have led with that. But I'm still processing everything myself." He hesitated. "What I mean is, give me some slack here as it's a tricky situation to and even more difficult to explain it."

Everyone nodded, so he continued.

"Eriel has been taken into custody by the archangels. He betrayed them, and has betrayed us. He's no longer a threat to us, but he's compromised our mission. Problem is, we don't know how much. But we do know more about his intentions – to gain control of the earth by any means possible. Going up against the archangels to do it, that was taking some kind of risk – even when he had The Furies on his side."

An audible gasp from everyone caused him to pause for a moment or two before he continued.

"The archangels have turned their backs on him. I met Michael, who leads the archangels, and he was disgusted with Eriel. And Eriel was terrified of him."

More audible gasps.

"Our Plan A was to trap The Furies within the gaming environment. Eriel was aware of this plan. In fact, he encouraged us to go ahead with it. So, we need to move on to Plan B. The very fact that he knew about Plan A, is enough for us to discard it."

More gasps and an "Oh no!"

"So, Plan B. I know you're thinking the obvious thing: i.e., we don't have a Plan B. Well, we didn't. But we do now. Will it shock you to know, that our Plan B has come from the mouth of our betrayer?"

All nodded.

"Like I said previously, I met with Michael. It was him, who suggested to Eriel, that leniency may be placed upon him, if and only if, he helped us.

"Michael only gave us five minutes together. And for the majority of that time Eriel said nothing. Then, just as it was about to expire, he said three words: "Use Raphael's glasses" – that was it. I remembered sometime later that Raphael had said Charles could be our secret weapon, so with the glasses we might have two weapons they have no knowledge of."

Charles gasped.

E-Z acknowledged Charles with a nod.

"But before we narrow it down and do some brainstorming, we need to look at the big picture here and decide if this is our fight. If this is something we still want to, as a team be involved in.

"Because of Eriel, I am alive today. He saved me and then said I owed him and the other archangels. To repay this debt I completed several trials. Alfred and Lia came along and together we formed The Three. And then we parted at their request.

"We set up our own superhero website and we helped people. Until the archangels requested our help to defeat the Soul Catcher pirates. In time we learned who they were: The Furies, powerful and evil Greek goddesses who'd returned.

"Hadz and Reiki took me on some reconnoitering, to show me their headquarters in Death Valley. There I saw for myself the stockpiling of containers filled with the souls of children. Later, PJ and Arden were taken from us. Their condition hasn't changed. And we saw firsthand, thanks to Raphael, those nasty goddesses at work.

"The Furies are worthy opponents. If we fight them, we could die. This of course isn't latest information but is it worth risking our lives for now that Eriel has betrayed us?

"Taking everything into consideration, and especially, that we have two secret weapons on our side. Albeit weapons which we don't know how we can use. Perhaps, we are in a good situation to win this fight. That's if we stick together and if we have each other's backs. If we are willing to put our lives on the line still for the greater good. For the good of the earth, saving the earth. What say ye?"

Next thing he knew everyone – except for Alfred – was bouncing around on the bed saying, "One for all and all for one!"

E-Z raised his hand. "

"All in favour of fighting The Furies, say, Aye."

The decision was unanimous.

Sobo knocked on the door asking, "Perhaps, I can help, too."

CHAPTER 17

ASK CHARLES DICKENS

BRANDY SCOFFED AUDIBLY CAUSING everyone in the room to look in her direction. Now that she had everyone's attention she asked, "And how are you, a senior citizen, going to help our team of superheroes kids to beat the three powerful evil goddesses?"

A gasp rang throughout the room, causing Haruto move quickly to the side of his Sobo. He grabbed her hand and held it against his heart.

Sobo who wasn't fazed by Brandy's ignorance whispered soothing words in Japanese to her grandson.

"Apologize," E-Z demanded.

"It's okay," Sobo said. "She's right, I may not be a superhero like all of you, but everyone in this life has something to give."

"Sorry, Sobo," Brandy said. She didn't stop there. "What I meant was..."

"Zip it!" Lia exclaimed. "Come on in Sobo."

"We can use all the help we can get," E-Z said.

Charles stood, offering his place to Sobo and Haruto.

"Thank you," Sobo said, and she and her grandson sat side by side without speaking for a few moments.

"Are you feeling well enough?" Haruto asked.

"Yes, little one, Sobo said. "I, too, have a superpower. That superpower is called transformation. I have lived many lives, and played many parts...with each life I learn something new. I'm open to learning, it's what life is about. I am offering my life; I'd do anything to save you. All of you."

"Even me?" Brandy asked.

Sobo laughed. "Especially you, child."

Brandy crossed the room and threw her arms around Sobo's neck. "Thank you. But why especially me?"

Haruto stood and with his hands on his hips exclaimed, "Because you're a nutter!"

Everyone laughed, including Brandy.

Sobo said, "Because you're fearless. Yes, being fearless is a powerful emotion, but you must learn patience. You need both, to survive in this world. With both you'll become even more of a force to reckon with. Life is about changing, yourself from the inside to the outside, from the outside to the inside. Learn. Grow. We must be like the trees, changing with the seasons, bending with the wind."

"So beautiful," Charles said.

"But the world is filled with both good and evil," Sobo said. "It has to be that way. One must exist for the other to be. And we, you and I and everyone here, we must only fight for the side of the good. In this world there can only be one winner. That winner must be for the good of all humankind."

Sobo stopped speaking. While she caught her breath, the others remained quiet waiting for her to continue.

"Why I am here," Sobo continued, "is to bring greetings from Rosalie."

"You and Rosalie, Sobo, but how?" Lia inquired.

"Rosalie came to me in a dream. How did I know it was she? Because she told me so. Dreams are powerful uniters. Spirits cross worlds and mingle with us to be with us, or to tell us things we do not know such as warnings, premonitions. Rosalie wanted to help us fight the battle, to fight and win."

"Yes," E-Z said. "I often dream of my parents. Sometimes they reveal things to me, or tell me things which they couldn't know about. Unless they were sharing my life with me."

"Yes, love is a powerful emotion which has no boundaries. Those who you love will seek you, find you, help you, even in the most darkest of times."

"Is she," Lia asked, "happy?"

Sobo smiled. "Happiness is not all. Let me just tell you, she is herself. That is all you really need to know. And as herself, as a vessel who fights on the side of only the good too, she believes in you, Mr. Charles Dickens. You are our power."

"Me?" Charles asked.

"Yes, Charles. Take us to the library. The library in the clouds."

"I've never heard of it. I can't take you there. She must've mixed me up with one of the others."

"What library?" Brandy asked.

"And why is it in the clouds?" Lia inquired.

"I've been there," Sobo said. "It's very old and it's protected...only those who know know."

"I'm not one of them," Charles said.

"You just need a little help," Sobo said. "Give him Raphael's glasses and he will then, be in the know."

"Wait a minute," E-Z said. "How did you get there?"

"Don't you believe me?" Sobo smiled. "Rosalie took me there in a dream...she's a spirit...and she led me as a dream walker."

"Are you sure it wasn't a memory she was sharing about The White Room?"

"Definitely not. How do I know this?" Sobo asked. "Because Rosalie told me she never wanted to return to the place where she was murdered by those vicious sisters."

"That makes sense, and yet, something Raphael said about never handing over the glasses – to anyone – makes me worried about going against her wishes."

"What if Rosalie is not one of those who are in the know?" Sobo inquired. "Are we meant to pass up this opportunity to increase our odds against defeating The Furies by rejecting latest information by Rosalie a trusted friend and confidante?"

"Tell me first," E-Z said, "what was it like?"

Sobo closed her eyes. "Imagine a time when you turned on the hot water only in a shower or bath, with no fan and no window open. You left the room to get something and closed the door. When you opened it later, the room was filled with steam and when you entered you couldn't see anything – at first. But your eyes adjusted and then you could see everything. It was the same for me when I first entered in the Cloud Library."

She opened her eyes. "Imagine the interior of the cloud where books existed. Every single book written, published all there in front of you. Available to read, to take, to learn. That is what it was like in the Cloud Library. And we're all meant to go and see it for ourselves, now. Today."

"It sounds magical," Charles said. "I want to go. I want to take you all there."

"It sounds too good to be true," Brandy said.

Sobo smiled.

E-Z hesitated before removing the glasses and handing them to Charles.

"E-Z," Sobo said, "Rosalie told me the exception to Raphael's rule was Charles. Remember? And she was the one who revealed that Charles was our secret weapon."

E-Z nodded and gave the glasses to Charles.

Without hesitation, Charles put them on. As he tucked them in behind his ears, the colours on the frames pulsated in every colour known to man. All colours except for red. When the glasses settled into grass shade of green, Charles' neck twisted left right left right left. He straightened up, stared ahead.

"I'm ready," he said. "Hold hands, so we're all connected, and I'll take you there."

"Wait for us!" Hadz and Reiki cried, as they jumped onto E'Z shoulders and held on for dear life. Moments later and no one had gone anywhere.

CHAPTER 18

WHAT WENT WRONG?

"I DON'T GET IT," Charles said. "I could see it in my mind. Maybe I need instructions, or some magic words. Did Rosalie tell you anything special I needed to do besides put the glasses on Sobo?" Charles inquired.

Sobo shook her head. "Try something different."

"Take us to The Cloud Room!" he demanded.

This time as a group all swayed, like someone had opened a window.

"Close your eyes," Charles said. "Everyone ready?" All nodded. He closed his eyes as the group of superheroes plus Sobo fragmented.

"Something feels, different," Lachie said opening his eyes. "I feel different."

E-Z also felt strange, as he opened his eyes. Hadz and Reiki were snoring now. Seemed a strange time for them to take a nap. And, what else was different? Raphael's glasses were colour-less. Why? It had never happened before. And what else? Alfred – where the heck was Alfred?

"Alfred? Where are you?"

Lia burst into tears.

"Why are you crying?" E-Z asked.

"Because I can't see anything, not with my hands. Not anymore."

"Charles. The glasses," Brandy said.

"What about the?" he removed them.

They covered their ears, as Sobo threw back her head and wailed like a banshee, until the soft orchestral music overpowered her cries, and everyone fell asleep.

***

Now that the twins were sleeping, Samantha and Sam wondered how the meeting was going in E-Z room. When they arrived, the door was locked, and no one answered when they knocked.

"That's strange," Sam said. "E-Z never locks the door.

"Get the key," Samantha said.

Sam had a bad feeling, as he inserted the key into the lock.

Sam and Samantha looked on, as Sobo, Brandy, Lia, Lachie, Haruto, Charles and E-Z stared ahead like mannequins in a shop window.

"They're barely breathing," Sam said.

"And where's Alfred?"

"And why is Charles wearing Raphael's glasses?"

"I'm frightened," Samantha said, taking her husband's hand into hers.

"I don't think we should disturb anything here," Sam said. "I get the feeling something is going on we don't know about."

"It's creepy."

"What's that?" Sam asked, noticing the box at the end of E-Z's bed. "I don't believe it! It can't be." He bent down, lifted the lid of the chest he'd seen many times in his brother's room. A chest which he'd thought had been destroyed in the fire. As had happened with E-Z, the memories created by the scents inside rose up and he was overwhelmed with emotions.

"Let's get out of here," Samantha said. "You can tell me more about the chest, outside."

"Let's give it a bit of time. They'll wake up soon and..."

"I don't think we have any other choice," Samantha said, as they closed the door behind them.

CHAPTER 19
THE CLOUD ROOM

CHARLES STOOD FOR A moment, taking in his surroundings. Had he brought them to the wrong place? He and the others (who were all sleeping) were high in the sky, without a single cloud in sight. They had landed in the middle of a platform made of glass. How it was being held up, he had no idea. He noticed E-Z's wheelchair was rolling forward, so rushed over and woke him up.

"Where are we?" he asked, flicking Hadz and Reiki who were still on his shoulders sound asleep awake.

"Wake up! Wake up!" Charles commanded.

One by one they opened their eyes, then realizing how high up they were, they clung to each other, trying not to move. Trying not to look down through the pane of glass which was stopping them from crashing to the ground.

"Wish this thing had a railing!" Lia exclaimed. She could see everything now but a part of her wished she couldn't.

"What's holding it up, that's what I can't figure out," Charles said.

"I never was a b-big fan of heights," Brandy said, as she grabbed the nearest available hand to hers which belonged to Charles.

"Oh," he said, feeling how cold her hand was.

"I'm going to fly over there and take a look," E-Z said, and off he flew, moving around the platform which seemed like it grew out of thin air with nothing holding it up and no anchor keeping it in place.

Haruto held onto his Grandmother's hand. She was more slow to wake than the others. When she seemed fully awake, "Oh no," was all she said. Over and over again.

"This isn't The Cloud Room Rosalie took you to, is it?" Charles asked.

Sobo took one step, two steps, while the children clung to her. She closed her eyes, squeezed them tightly shut, then opened them again.

"What are you doing?" Brandy inquired.

"I'm looking for the books," Sobo said. "If this is the place, then there ought to be books. Lots of books. I can't see any. Not a one."

E-Z who was still investigating the structure of the platform, asked, "Does it feel like we're in the right place? Could the books be disguised? Can anyone see them?"

Everyone shook their heads in a no, even Hadz and Reiki who up to this point hadn't uttered a single word between the two of them.

"I have a bad, bad feeling about this place," Hadz and Reiki sang in unison.

Charles hesitated before speaking. "I saw a library in my head when I put the glasses on, and it was how Sobo described it to us. There was no glass platform. This place isn't the one I envisioned. At first, I thought the glasses had made an error, but now, if Hadz and Reiki have a bad feeling, and so does Sobo, I think." Sobo nodded, and he noticed she was trembling. "I think we need to get the heck out of here – and fast."

E-Z noticed Alfred was missing. "Anyone know what happened to Alfred? We were all connected by touch when we came here. How could he have become attached?" Now he noticed that Hadz and Reiki seemed out of it. Almost like they'd been drugged, as their eyes lolled back in their heads, and they were having difficulty in staying awake.

"Swans don't have fingers to touch," the two wannabe angels sang in unison. They they broke into laughter and spun around in circles until they were too dizzy to remain afloat and they dropped down onto the glass floor with a SPLAT.

"Okay Charles, that's enough evidence for me. Take us back home again – now."

Charles who had removed Raphael's glasses, now put them back on again with the intention of following E-Z's orders exclaimed, "Oh, there they are!"

"You can see the books now?" Sobo asked.

"I couldn't when we first arrived, but now I can. Now what am I supposed to do?"

"It makes no sense," Sobo said, "why would they be disguised to you, then revealed? Rosalie didn't mention these things."

"I think the air up here is affecting our brains," E-Z said. "I'm beginning to feel out of it, lightheaded. We better get out of here and pronto or we'll wind up face down on the platform like Hadz and Reiki."

Charles held his hand out and a book flew into it which he stuffed inside his shirt. "Take us back!" he cried. As the first time they tried it, nothing happened.

"Perhaps we need to hold hands," Sobo said. "And close our eyes again."

They did both and immediately, huge gusts of wind began to blow them about on the platform. They huddled, like a football team before a big play, clinging to each other. Pushing their feet onto the platform, in hope they wouldn't fly away.

E-Z wracked his brain, trying to think of a way out. Was the only way using the one and only chance to summon Raphael to come to the rescue? He looked over at Charles, who seemed to be fading in and out. "Charles!" he screamed, and then he noticed, over his shoulder, coming toward them fast were Baby, Little Dorrit and Alfred.

Alfred screamed, "We've got to get you out of here – now. This place is like a beacon, lighting you up for the entire world to see, including The Furies!"

Sobo sobbed, "I didn't know they used Rosalie as a trap."

"Charles did see the books, and he even got one. Let's get ourselves to safety. No one is to blame. Your intentions were all good," E-Z said.

"Thank you," Sobo said, as she began to fade in and out, like Charles had. Brandy took hold of her hand, and held it tightly until Sobo no longer faded.

Alfred said, "Come on!"

Lachie jumped up on Baby's back, pulling the trembling Charles aboard with him and off they flew. Inside his shirt, the book he was holding there expanded and two of his shirt buttons flew off. He held the book firmly with one arm, and onto Lachie with the other as Baby picked up the pace.

Little Dorrit bowed down without touching the platform, so the rest could get on board, while E-Z grabbed Hadz and Reiki. Off they flew, with Alfred and E-Z flying side by side, as the sky changed from blue to black, black to blue, to black, and the stars came out, but they weren't stars. They were eyeballs. Booger firing eyeballs, like the ones he'd encountered in Death Valley when he'd first encountered The Furies.

SPLAT. SPLAT. SPLAT.

SPLAT. SPLAT. SPLAT. SPLAT.

SPLAT. SPLAT. SPLAT. SPLAT. SPL-

Charles screamed at the top of his lungs, "HOME!" And this time it worked. They were home again. Safe.

Haruto threw his arms around his grandmother.

"So glad to be back home again," each said to the other.

Moments later, Sam and Samantha arrived.

$$* * *$$

"WE SAW YOUR BODIES asleep in your room. We didn't know what to do," Sam said.

"It's a long story," E-Z said.

Sobo asked Charles, "Did you manage to keep a hold of the book?""Sure did," Charles said, holding it up. It was a large volume, hardback, with a thick spine which could be see and read by all –

Great Expectations by Charles Dickens.

"You brought back one of your own books?" Brandy exclaimed.

Lachie scoffed.

"I..." Charles said. "You told me to pick any book, and this was the one I grabbed at random."

"Everything happens for a reason," Lia said.

"But this is really stretching it," Brandy exclaimed.

"Everyone calm down," E-Z said. "Charles did his best under the circumstances – and at least HE could see the books. None of us could."

"Great Expectations," Alfred said, "is a grrr-eat book!" He sounded like the British version of Tony the Tiger on the cereal commercials.

"He's right," Sam and Samantha agreed. "It is one of the finest novels ever written."

Charles removed Raphael's glasses and handed them back to E-Z who immediately put them on. He shook his head, but the title of the book Charles was holding still was different. He read the new title aloud,

"Field of Dreams by W. P. Kinsella."

"Let me try," Lia said, reaching for Raphael's glasses.

"Wait!" E-Z cried, as Lia removed them from his face. "Don't put them on. Remember, Raphael said only I should wear them, but I made an exception for Charles because of Sobo's dream but I don't think we should pass them around. Besides, we already know the answer to the question we're all asking ourselves. It's a book that becomes whatever title the reader wants to see."

"Or needs to see," Sobo said.

"But I didn't want or need to see Great Expectations. I've never even heard of it!"

"But imagine," Sam said, "what kind of library it could be in the future. All we have to do is think up a book's title, and voila, we're holding it in our hands."

"Wouldn't be very good for the authors though, I mean how would they get paid?" Samantha inquired.

"I don't know how it would all work, and maybe we're missing something big here," Alfred said.

"Big, like what?" E-Z inquired.

"What if it was the book, who chose the reader instead of the other way around?"

"Doo-doo-doo-doo," Brandy sang which was the music from The Twilight Zone.

"Let's recap. Sobo had a dream in which Rosalie showed her The Cloud Library and with Raphael's glasses Charles could take us there. Which he did, but the place wasn't as expected. Only Charles could see the books, he grabbed one and, on the way, back we were attacked by booger shooting eyeballs similar to ones which attacked Hadz Reiki and I in Death Valley.""That's it in a nutshell," Brandy said.

"What I'm wondering is, did Eriel tell The Furies about Raphael giving E-Z her glasses," Lachie asked.

"That's something we might not ever know," E-Z said, "because Michael only gave Eriel one chance to talk to me." He went to the window and looked out. "I wonder," he said.

"Wonder what?" everyone exclaimed.

"If The Furies know about the glasses, and their powers. If they tricked us through Rosalie to visit The Cloud Library, then they must know about Charles. That means he is no longer a secret weapon. How could they possibly have known? And yet, the eye boogers – that's too much of a coincidence."

"Eriel did tell you to use the glasses," Alfred said.

"I saw him, how he was being detained and there was no way, no way possible he could have messaged The Furies...not with Michael guarding his every move." E-Z rolled back where the others were. "By the way Alfred, how did you get separated from us?"

"I was lost inside a black cloud, until I called for Little Dorrit and Baby to help me and you know the rest."

"It was so weird," Charles said. "One minute I couldn't see the books, I removed the glasses, put them back on again and they were everywhere. Still, I was the only one who could see them."

"I could see them" Baby said. "This one flew toward me," he tossed it to Charles who caught it with two fingers.

It was a miniature book, with a tiny title on the spine which everyone read aloud:

"Everything You Ever Wanted to Know About The Furies But Were Afraid To Ask by Anonymous."

"Score!" Brandy exclaimed.

They gathered around the tiny book, while Charles every so carefully opened it. Inside the front cover was blank, as was the first page. He turned to the next page, where there were words, which immediately began to move around, to shuffle. The words floated around on the page, shuffling, and reshuffling like they'd forgotten what words and language they were meant to represent.

E-Z who was still wearing Raphael's glasses felt dizzy as the words shifted around, and he took them off.

"You try," he said to Charles, handing the glasses over.

Charles put them on and quickly removed them again, rushing to the window for some fresh air. He handed them back to E-Z.

"Now you," he said to Sobo, who refused to try the glasses on as did Haruto."

"I'll give it a go," Lia said, but she soon joined Charles at the window.

"Lachie?" E-Z asked.

"Sure thing," he said, putting the glasses on, then immediately taking them off again. "No go," he said, plopping down onto the bed.

"Let me have a go!" Brandy said, as E-Z put the glasses into her hand, and she applied them to her face. "Wait a minute," she said, "I think I see something, it's it's..." and she spewed a green substance which fortunately hit the wall instead of a person.

"Come with us," Sam and Samantha said to Brandy, "we'll help you get cleaned up."

"Uh, thanks," E-Z said, turning his chair toward Alfred, then placing the glasses upon his beak.

"A swan wearing glasses. Ridiculous!" Alfred said.

"You look very studious!" Charles said.

"You look like Professor Ludwig Von Drake!" Brandy exclaimed.

Sam said, "He was Donald Duck's teacher."

"Oh," those who were too young to have heard of Donald Duck said.

"Oh my," Alfred said, as the words stopped swirling and returned to the way in which the author had written them. He read the first two page, then the next, the next and the next. He flew through the entire book with the ease of a speed reader and when he was finished, the book slammed itself shut.

POOF

And it was gone.

"Well, that was interesting," Alfred said, handing the glasses back to E-Z and stopping himself from falling over.

"You mean you read the whole thing?" Sam said. "Those glasses are remarkable."

"I recall everything, but I need to process the information and I need to rest. I don't want to sit here and read it back to you in its entirety. It's better if I sort through what I've learned and then we'll talk about it."

"What if," Brandy asked, "you missed something one of us wouldn't have missed? Nothing personal."

Alfred laughed. "Just because I'm in the form of a swan now, it doesn't mean I haven't read many, many books in my lifetime. In fact, I attended Oxford University when I was a young man and graduated with honours. I've studies Literature and the Arts."

E-Z said, "You didn't choose the book – the book chose you. None of us could read a single word in it."

"Thank you, for believing in me."

Lia said, "How much time do you want to mull? We can go and watch that movie?"

Samantha said, "I'll need to make some more popcorn. We already ate the other bowlful."

"Stress eating," Sam said with a smirk.

"Thanks," Alfred said. "I'll be back to you, as soon as I can."

"Take all the time you need," E-Z said, "come and join us when you're ready."

The gang went into the living area and got the movie ready. Samantha made some more popcorn in the microwave. Everyone gathered around to watch the movie.

Alfred slept for a while in his usual place, but he dreamed dreams, mostly nightmares and eventually took himself into the garden and get some fresh air. Everyone was depending up on him, and the pressure weighed down on him, as the contents of the miniature book swirled around in his mind.

CHAPTER 20

MESSAGE FROM FRANCE

E-Z WATCHED THE FIRST half of the movie with the others, then feeling restless he decided to catch up on some work. He popped his head into his room, expecting to find Alfred sound asleep but he was nowhere to be found. Concerned, he went to the back door and looked out to see the swan sound asleep stretched out on a lawn chair. He closed the door and returned to his room and flipped open his laptop and logged in.

He went back and forth in his mind a few times, deciding if he could concentrate on writing his novel, or whether he should spend this time doing more research on their enemies The Furies. The sound of a message which pinged into his inbox made the decision for him. It had a red tick, denoting urgency and even though it did not contain attachments he didn't click on it. Instead, he read it in preview. Or, tried to read it. The message was entirely in a different language. He spotted a couple of words he recognized as French, so he copied the text, went onto a search engine, and pasted the following message into an online translator:

Cher E-Z Dickens,

Je m'appelle François Dubois et j'ai sept ans. J'habite à Paris, en France, et j'aimerais faire partie de votre équipe de Superhéros. Vous vous demandez peut-être quelles compétences j'apporterais à l'équipe. C'est une bonne question et je serai heureux d'y répondre. Mais je me demande si ce site est sécurisé.

Si vous souhaitez me parler davantage, vous pouvez m'envoyer un courriel directement. Mon adresse de courriel est jointe. J'ai hâte d'avoir de vos nouvelles.

Votre ami,

Francois

He pushed send and the following translation came through:

Dear E-Z Dickens,

My names in Francois Dubois and I am seven years old. I live in Paris, France, and I would like to be on your Superhero team. You might ask what skills I would bring to the team. It's a good question and I'm happy to answer it. But I wonder, is this site secure?

If you would like to speak with me more, you can email me directly. My email address is attached. I look forward to hearing from you.

Your friend,

Francois

Intrigued, he reread the message several times, thinking about the timing of it. Wondering if he was being paranoid in thinking this kid all the way from France could be conspiring with The Furies. Even if he was being over-cautious, he had a right to be and as the leader of his team, it was up to him make sure inquiries like this were legit. He'd need Uncle Sam's help to check into it, but for now, he'd put out a few feelers and see what came back.

He wrote a quick message without translating it. The kid could use a search engine, the same as he did and find a translator and after re-reading it several times pushed SEND.

Dear Francois,

Thank you for your message. How did you hear about us?Sincerely,

E-Z.

Francois' reply came back so fast it made E-Z feel even more suspicious. This time in English it read:

Dear E-Z,

Thank you for your quick reply.

My teacher saw your website, and we learned about you and your team as part of our current events lesson.

Hope to hear from you soon.

Your friend,

Francois.

It certainly sounded legit. He typed in another message, asking Francois what kind of superhero powers he had to offer his team so he could discuss it with them. Moments later Francois sent him the following message:

Dear E-Z,

Thank you for giving you the opportunity to tell you about my superhero skills.

First, like you, I haven't always been a superhero. This is something we have in common. That's why I thought I would be a good fit for your team.

Instead of telling you, I'd like to show you. Attached is a private invitation to view our YouTube Channel – my dad helped me. The link it only available to you and the invitation to view will expire in twenty-four-hours.

I look forward to hearing from you after you've seen it.

Your friend,

Francois.

Curious and without hesitation E-Z clicked on the link. A message popped up asking him to answer a question which he had no problem answering since it was baseball related.

Once in, he clicked on the clip, turned up the volume and it immediately started.

The first person he saw, was a kid who introduced himself as seven-year-old Francois Dubois via the text which was translated from him at the bottom of the screen.

The kid was tall, very tall. In fact, he was standing beside several measuring sticks. His father zoomed in to show that Francois, at seven year's old he was already 163 centimeters (5 ft. 4 in.) tall. Besides his height, Francois looked like any other seven-year-old, with reddish-brown hair, a thick pair of glasses with dark rims on his nose, a plaid shirt, blue jeans, and black runners.

"Bonjour E-Z!" Francois said, beaming a smile which revealed his two front teeth were missing.

E-Z smiled back, then watched as Francois and his father discussed a matter in French without any translation provided. Their discussion seemed heated, based upon their hand gestures and facial expressions. He hoped Francois wasn't going to attempt something dangerous.

E-Z watched as Francois continued walking to the most well-known landmark of Paris, France - The Eiffel Tower. A sign outside indicated cost for enter was for those aged 12-24 years was 5 euros. Francois closed his eyes, then opened them again. Wait a minute. Something had changed, perhaps it was the lighting.

He continued watching as Francois positioned himself alongside of a different sign which read:

Paris World Fair, May 15, 1889.

"WHOA!" E-Z exclaimed, trying to figure out what he'd just witnessed. Time travel?

Francois closed his eyes and was back beside the original sign 12-24 years 5 euros.

The camera went all fuzzy. Along the bottom of the screen the words appeared, "One moment please."

With a click, the camera started rolling again, but this time, Francois was standing beside the Notre-Dame de Paris Cathedral. Since the great fire of 2019, it was being rebuilt and the scaffolding and cranes were busily working.

As before, Francois closed his eyes then reopened them.

"No way!" E-Z exclaimed.

Francois was in 1163 on the very day in which the first stone for the great Notre Dame Cathedral was put in place.

E-Z hit pause. Could this be fake? Of course, it could. With today's technology anyone could fake anything. And yet something in his gut told him it was legit. He needed a second opinion though. He needed Uncle Sam.

Looking at the paused Francois on screen, E-Z clicked start. Francois waved as the clip ended.

E-Z clicked and returned to his inbox. He pushed reply and wrote the following email to Francois:

Dear Francois,

Thanks for letting me see your superpower. I need to talk to the team. If we decide to accept you, how soon can you join us?

Your friend,

E-Z

He waited for a second and reread his message before hitting send. He considered changing IF to WHEN. Undecided, he considered Francois time travelling superpower. The kid would be an amazing addition to the team.

Still, he had to get a second opinion. Before thought about it any further. He texted Sam, "Have you got a sec?"

A new email popped into his mailbox with the words:

HI E-Z,

If you accept me onto the team, can you come and get me?

Your friend,

Francois.

That he had to do some thinking about.

He replied:

Will be back to you asap.

Your friend,

E-Z.

Sam entered the kitchen, "What's up kiddo?"

"Sorry to take you away from the movie."

"I was nodding off anyway so glad for the distraction."

"I received an email via our website from a kid in France who asked to join our team. He and his dad made a clip, I've already watched it. He has impressive skills. Take a look and let me know what you think."

Sam remained quiet throughout. When it ended, he asked to see it again.

When it finished for the second time E-Z asked, "What do you think?"

"I think what we see is impressive. A time travelling boy from France."

"We could really use a superpower like that on our team."

"Exactly," Sam said. "And that's why I'm suspicious about it. Have you corresponded with the lad?"

E-Z scrolled through what had been said thus far.

"How does he know that you haven't had superpowers all your life?" he asked.

"Yeah, that's what I thought too. But I think it's a reasonable assumption. He's a smart kid."

"True," Sam said. "Mind if I click around, see what I can find?"

E-Z nodded, and Sam took control of his laptop. He checked the IP address which seemed to be legit. He had no trouble tracking its location in Paris.

He searched Francois' name, found out what school he attended. Found out he played basketball. Found out he was clever at spelling. Didn't seem to get himself into trouble.

Then Sam found a death notice for Francois' mother who had died when he was five. Cause of death was not specified, but donations were requested to be made to the Paris Breast Cancer Foundation.

"Everything seemed to be legit," Sam said.

"Still, how can we be certain? I don't want to take any unnecessary risks."

"The only way to know for certain, would be to interview the kid in person." He hesitated, "Hm, he asked when you can come and collect him. Now that I think about it, that's rather an odd think for a time travelling kid to suggest."

"Yeah, I hadn't thought about it like that."

"One thing's for certain E-Z, if anyone is going to get him, it will be me. You're needed here."

"I appreciate the offer Uncle Sam but your life in danger isn't an option."

"Okay," Sam said. "Have you heard anything from Alfred?"

On cue Alfred waddled into the kitchen. "WHAT?" he asked.

ZAP

A tiny white fluffy kitten arrived.

"Bonjour E-Z, je m'appelle Poppet. Francois m'envoie."

"Oh boy," was all E-Z said.

Immediately an email from Francois pinged which read:

"Did she get there safely?"

Uncle Sam said, "Well, that answers our question."

E-Z typed in, "Yes, she's here."

ZAP

Poppet disappeared.

"This is so cool," Francois typed. "When you're ready, if you want me on your team, I'll give it a try myself."

"Hold tight for now," E-Z said.

"How did Poppet know where we lived?" Sam inquired.

"That I do not know."

CHAPTER 21

THE FRANCOIS DECISION

THE NEXT DAY, E-Z called an emergency group meeting. Once everyone was seated, he got straight into it.

"A potential new member has asked to join our team. Sam and I have investigated his application and everything looks legit."

"I second that opinion," Sam said.

E-Z nodded, "Francois is a time traveler."

"Wow!" Lia said.

"Awesome!" Lachie said.

The others had similar comments with the exception of Charles who asked, "What's a time traveler?"

"You are!" Brandy said.

"It's someone who travels from one time to another," Lia said.

"Perhaps just have a look at this clip, and you'll get a better understanding, we'll all get a better understanding of what he can do." He glanced at Alfred, "But, before we talk about Francois, I'd like to hand the floor over to Alfred, so he can fill us in on what he discovered in the book. Over to you, Alfred."

The trumpeter swan cleared his throat, as all eyes turned toward him.

"I went over everything, frontwards, backwards, sideways and I'm afraid it's not much help. Since The Furies were given a specific mandate – and they are adhering to it (even though they are bending the rules) I don't even think Zeus could punish them for what they are doing."

"Are you saying it's hopeless?" Brandy asked.

"No, I'm not saying it's hopeless, but I just can't see a way out. That is, unless they don't know what we know."

"Which is?" Brandy asked.

"Eriel's plan. How he was using them. Where Eriel is. How he is incommunicado."

"True, they must be wondering why he's not communicating with them," Lachie said.

"And that could create distrust," Brandy added.

"What if," Sam said, "that information was leaked to them?""I was thinking the same thing," Samantha said. "Maybe without him, they'd turn tail and run."

"It might go the opposite way though. Without him keeping them on a leash, they might. Well, who knows what they'd do!" E-Z said.

"They've already collected a lot of souls," Lia said. "I think E-Z is right. Knowing he's out of the picture could make them bolder."

Alfred noticed the conversation was hitting a wall, "So, let's talk about Francois' superpower skills. He's a time traveler. How could he help us?"

"One more thing," E-Z began, "and it's Uncle Sam who noticed this so perhaps he would be the best person to explain it."

"No, you go ahead," Sam said.

"Francois sent a kitten here."

"A kitten?" Sobo asked.

"Yes. Her name was Poppet, and she arrived in the kitchen. I received a message from Francois straight away asking if she arrived safely. She said hello – yes, she could talk. Upon confirmation she'd arrived safely, she popped out again. The question Sam posed later was, how did she know where we lived?"

"Wait a minute," Charles said. "Didn't someone tell me your address was published online?"

"I heard that too," Brandy said.

Sam said, "Wow that seems like ages ago, but it's true."

They gathered around Sam and saw their house online connected to the website for everyone in the world to see.

"Well, there's no doubt about it. If they know who we are, then they also know where we are," Sam said. "Unless..."

"Unless what?" E-Z asked.

"Unless they aren't as tech savvy as we think they are."

Sobo said, "Never underestimate an enemy. That's how unworthy villains become heroes."

"Okay, first let's watch Francois time travelling and then let's do some brainstorming about how he could help us defeat The Furies," E-Z said.

They watched the clip in silence. When it ended, E-Z said, "I'll type out the list. Who wants to start?"

"No," Sam said. "I think we should write it down the old-fashioned way. You know, with pen and paper." He reached into the kitchen drawer and pulled out a notepad they used for grocery lists, and a pen. "You go ahead and brainstorm, I'll be the secretary. And you don't even have to pay me a salary."

A few laughs and sniggers then ideas began to flow:

#1. Francois could go back in time, find out what happened to PJ and Arden and stop it.

#2. Francois could go back in time and stop all the kids from being killed.

#3. Francois could go back in time and stop E-Z's parents from being killed, stop his accident from happening.

#4. Ditto re: Lia's accident.

#5. Ditto re: Alfred's family's accident.

#6. Ditto re: Lachlan being locked in a cage.

Interlude.

Haruto was happy with his new family. End of story.

Brandy was fine with being able to die and come back to life again although she did inquire whether going back to audition day was a viable option. This request was unanimously denied.

Charles also had no regrets.

Brainstorming session resumed:

#7. Francois could go back to the time before The Furies were created to ensure they were given an Achilles Heel.

#8. Francois could go back in time, to the first day Eriel met with The Furies. He could be a spy. Or could he make sure they never met at all?

#9. If Poppet could pop in and out could Francois do the same?

Alfred said, "Wait a minute. This is completely crazy, but what if Francois went back and cancelled The Furies out of existence."

"Wow that's an excellent idea!" E-Z said. "But in all the stories I've read about time travel, playing with lives and changing events is always frowned upon."

"Yeah, I remember that from Back to the Future. But from personal experience, " Brandy explained, "when I die and come back again, it's like the events leading up to my death never happened. It's like a dream, if you know what I mean?"

"Sam stretched and yawned. "The babies will be waking up soon. I don't want to overstep E-Z's leadership boundaries, but I think we need to spend some time thinking before we take any actions."

"Agreed. Thanks everyone for an excellent brainstorming session," E-Z said.

And the meeting was adjourned.

CHAPTER 22
WARM MILK

LIA AND THE OTHERS spent the day doing their own thing. In the evening, exhausted, she tossed and turned, but could not sleep. Frustrated after hours of no sleep and constant worrying, she went downstairs for a little warm milk.

She popped a mug into the microwave, hit 40 seconds, then pushed start. As the clock counted down, she watched the numbers 39, 38, 37, 36, etc., until the number 33 appeared. It was the last number she saw.

"Uh, hello Little Dorrit," she said, wishing she'd put on her robe. "Where are we off to?"

"We're on a mission," the unicorn said. "Where are we off to?"

"You don't know who?"

"No. I was minding my own business when you called for me Lia, don't you remember?"

"I didn't call you," Lia said. "I haven't been to sleep yet. This is strange."

The unicorn froze mid-air.

WHOOSH

Little Dorrit took off at full speed.

"Argghh!" Lia cried, holding on for dear life. "What's happening? Why are you going so fast?"

"I don't know," the unicorn said. "It's like someone or something has taken control of me." She tried to stop, as she'd done only moments before. Now, no matter what she did, she couldn't stop. Nor could she slow down.

"Hold on tightly!" Little Dorrit shouted, as her body began to roll forwards head over heels. "Oh no!"

Lia screamed, but held on for dear life. Eventually they stopped rolling, but rather than slowing down they sped up even faster.

On and on they flew as night turned into day. As the sun made its way up the sky the distance between it and them lessened.

"I feel like my skin is burning!" Lia exclaimed.

"So is my fur," Little Dorrit said. "Let me try turning us around again." She did try and as before they rolled head over heels, head over heels, closing the gap between them and the hot sun.

"We have to turn back!" Lia screamed. "If we don't, we're done for."

"But I can't seem to stop. I can't seem to do anything. Wait, I'll ask for Baby's help."

With the flaming sun as their backdrop, three winged creatures came into view. They held hands, as their blackened robes swirled and twisted around their bodies.

SNAP!

SNAP!

SNAP!

Was the sound which filled the air the sound of a whip snapping as Lia and Little Dorrit were pulled toward it like they were on a tractor beam. Thunder rolled, although no storms were visible as the sun's talons stretched toward them, threatening to disintegrate their very existence.

"We're done for!" Lia said. "Thank you for trying to save us." She hugged the unicorn. "I sure wish you had reins. Then maybe I could turn you around."

ZAP!

Reins appeared.

Lia wrapped her hands around them, but before she could take control of them, they melted into nothing.

"You're right, I think we're done for," Little Dorrit said. Glass teardrops flowed from her eyes.

BONJOUR

Francois appeared, "Might I be of assistance?"

"You sure can," Lia exclaimed. "Get us the heck out of here!"

"Close your eyes and hold on tight," Francois said.

Lia and Little Dorrit trembled with fear.

DING. DING. DING.

The microwave. The kitchen.

Lia dropped to the floor.

Little Dorrit landed safely in a cool stream, where she splashed around, then headed home.

"Where've you been?" Baby asked.

"Guess you didn't get my message. Never mind. I'm too tired," Little Dorrit said. "I'll tell you about it in the morning."

CHAPTER 23
NEXT DAY

IT WAS SOBO'S TURN to cook breakfast, it was she who found Lia, on the floor rolled up like a discarded ball of wool.

Sobo let out a scream, "Come quickly! Our Lia needs help!"

Samantha was the first to arrive. She immediately pressed her lips to Lia's forehead to check for a temperature, then yelled for her husband to bring to thermometer to double check.

"Her temperature is 107.7," Sam confirmed. "We need to get her to the hospital."

Samantha hit 911 while Sam picked Lia up and carried and placed her on the sofa and they waited for the ambulance.

"I'll hold down the fort," Sam said, as his wife and Sobo followed the paramedics who carried the unconscious Lia on a stretcher.

As the ambulance pulled away from the curb with siren blazing, Lia opened her eyes and tried to sit up.

"I feel fine," she said.

The paramedic checked her temperature again and it was normal. He shrugged his shoulders.

By the time they arrived at the hospital, Lia was back to her old self and wanting to go back home again – now.

"Although her vitals are fine now, since you called us, we need to follow through. Lia will be admitted, and once given the all-clear by the doctor on call, she'll be allowed to go home."

"Well, at least let me walk in," the attendee said, as the driver opened the doors.

"No, little lady you stay put," he said, as they prepared to bring the stretcher and its occupant inside with Samantha and Sobo following.

Samantha texted Sam an update. He replied with a thumb's up emoji, just as she practically walked into PJ and Arden's parents who were on the way out.

"They're awake! Our boys are awake!"

"Both of them?" Samantha exclaimed, as she relayed this latest information to Sam, who, woke his nephew to tell him the good news.

"Be right there!" E-Z said after calling a taxi.

CHAPTER 24
AT THE HOSPITAL

E-Z WAS ON THE way to see his two best friends. In the taxi, his mind kept repeating the good news over and over again. So much had happened. So much they'd missed. So many things he had to tell them. Wanted to tell them.

"Do you know which room?" the nurse asked.

He told her no, and she quickly found it for him. After thanking her, he caught the elevator and made his way to their room wondering if he should buy them something. Flowers? Candy. He decided to ask them if they needed anything.

Arriving just outside their door, inside he could hear their voices and he eaves dropped for a few moments, before making his presence known. Then he took a deep breath, trying to hold his emotions from overpowering him – he didn't want to get all mushy and embarrass himself...

"Come on in you big softy!" PJ said.

"Ahhhhh, he missed us!" Arden said.

"Shouldn't you guys be more good looking after all that beauty sleep? By the way, you both need a shave!"

"We don't want to overshadow you and I kind of life the feel of my stache," Arden said.

"We know you love the attention! I see your bottle brush could use a trim too!"

PJ's mother who'd just returned to the room whispered to E-Z that they didn't want the boys to overdo it, since they only been awake for a few hours.

After chatting a short while, E-Z hugged both his friends, and said he had to go. "I'll be back," he promised, "and I'll sneak in a burger or two – I've heard that hospital food is really really bad."

"You will not!" Arden's mother said as she also returned to the room.

He backed his chair up, with Arden's mother facing him, his two friends put their hands together, begging him to please bring them food.

As he made his way along the corridor, he couldn't believe how much he'd missed them – and how good they looked. He took the elevator down to Emergency where he found Samantha and Sobo.

"Any news?" E-Z asked.

"She was fine furious they were making her stay to check her out," Samantha said. "But I'll feel better once she gets the all clear and we can get out of here."

"Me too," E-Z said. "Let me go and have a look." He pushed along the corridor. Listening as he went to the voices inside a curtained area which he deemed to be pre-admission stations. Finally, he heard Lia's voice inside and went in.

"Please wait outside," the Nurse said.

"But she's my sister."

"I want to go home – now!" she demanded, then crossed her arms over her chest.

"You'll be discharged as soon as the doctor says you can be discharged. And not a moment sooner."

"How are you doing? Mom's worried about you."

"I'll leave the two of you alone to chat," the nurse said. "The doctor should be in very soon. Oh, and make sure she remains calm."

"Uh, thanks," E-Z said.

Once she was gone, they hugged.

"Little Dorrit and I nearly got burned up by the sun!" she said. She told E-Z everything, as it happened from start to finish.

"Interesting it was Francois who rescued you."

"I don't know how he knew. Little Dorrit and I thought we were a goner. It was definitely The Furies. They wanted to burn us up! We were getting singed. They are horrible, evil witches!"

"Were there snakes?" E-Z asked

"Snakes and whips."

"Sounds like The Furies all right." E-Z hesitated. He changed the subject. "Have you heard about PJ and Arden?"

She shook her head.

"They woke up!"

"No way! That's an odd coincidence don't you think? They try to take out Little Dorrit and I, meanwhile out two comatose friends wake up."

"You're right, I think it's all connected."

Samantha pushed back the curtain, "What's all connected?" She hugged her daughter. "How are you feeling now baby?"

"I'm not a baby," Lia said. "But I do feel better and I want to go home. After I visit with PJ and Arden."

Sobo came in. She hugged Lia.

"What happened to you?" she asked.

Again, Lia explained everything. Her mother didn't take it as well as Sobo did. E-Z rushed over and poured Sam a glass of water. Whereas Sobo had lots of questions. "You were warming milk, in the microwave?"

Lia nodded.

"And that's when you were zapped out of the kitchen?"

"Yes, and straight onto Little Dorrit's back. Little Dorrit said I'd summoned her, but I hadn't."

"And then what happened?" Sobo asked.

"Well, Little Dorrit was flying and were chatting and when neither of us knew where we were going or why, we were thinking about turning back. Next thing we knew, Little Dorrit and I were being forced nearer and nearer to the sun without any power to turn around."

"But you and Little Dorrit don't meet The Furies' criteria. They shouldn't be able to touch either of you!" E-Z exclaimed.

Samantha said, "Maybe it's just a coincidence.

Sobo repeated her advice from before, "Never underestimate an enemy."

Once Lia was cleared to go home, she and E-Z surprised PJ and Arden with cheeseburgers and fries which they smuggled in.

On the way home in the taxi, with Samantha, Sobo and Lia, E-Z was thinking one thing and one thing only. The Furies had attacked Lia and Little Dorrit and they'd failed. Not only had they failed – thanks to Francois – but somehow, someway, the universe had sent back PJ and Arden.

Coincidence? He thought not. Instead, what he wanted to believe, was that The Furies' powers diminished if they ventured outside their mandate.

Either way, he and his team had to be ready at any moment to take advantage of the situation.

This might be their only chance.

The only advantage in their favour.

CHAPTER 25

SOBO

"I HAVE TO ASK one more question," Sam asked E-Z before everyone came in for the meeting.

"Okay, ask away," E-Z said.

"Well, I wondered why Rosalie didn't know about Francois."

"I," was as far as E-Z got before Brandy and Lia came into the kitchen.

"Don't mind us," Brandy said, as she proceeded to open the refrigerator, take out the orange juice and finish it off before tossing the container into the recycling bin.

"Uh, you should rinse that out first," E-Z said, which Brandy did. Then she plunked down into a chair and wiped her mouth with the back of her hand.

"Sorry, I didn't mean to be rude, you know stopping abruptly as I did. I wanted us all to be here to discuss Uncle Sam's concerns."

"Fair enough," Lia said, taking a seat alongside of Brandy.

One by one the others arrived and took their places around the table.

E-Z began by updating everyone about PJ and Arden's miraculous recovery which was following by a rousing round of applause by all, including those who hadn't even met them yet.

"Next, on the agenda and I think these two items may be connected, Lia and Little Dorrit were tricked into leaving the house and their lives were put in danger. If it hadn't been for Francois, The Furies who we deem were responsible might have succeeded."

"Bravo Francois!" Charles said.

"How were you tricked?" Brandy inquired.

"Where did it happened?" Lachie asked.

"Lia, do you want to tell it?" E-Z asked. She shook her head, no. "Jump in if I miss anything," he said. He went ahead and explained what happened and why they thought The Furies were responsible.

"Since then, I've been thinking about The Furies and their mandate. As we know, they must follow it. When they tried to kill Lia and Little Dorrit, they broke the rules. What reason could they give, for trying to kill Lia, or Little Dorrit? Not only did they go against their mandate, but they failed. Now consider what happened at the exact same time – I mean of course PJ and Arden – they came out of their comas. Coincidence? I think not.

"And the more I connect them in my mind, the more I wonder if The Furies might be weakening. If I'm right, then now might be the right time for us to take them down."

"It's possible," Alfred said, "but I remember reading about Einstein back in my school days – which could prove otherwise. I mean, it might not have been The Furies at all. It might have been a disruption to the space-time continuum. Since Francois was able to save them, and none of us knew it was happening it seems a possibility worth investigating don't you think?"

Sam paced. "Given everything we know about The Furies, and what I remember from my studies about Einstein – to even have a chance at bending the space time continuum, Lia and Little Dorrit would have had to be travelling faster than light – 186,282 miles per second. If you were going that fast, you'd move backward in time not forward."

"We were travelling fast, but not that fast," Lia said.

"Tell us again what happened again Lia. Frame by frame. Right up to the time when Francois showed up," Alfred said.

Lia's story began in the kitchen and ended with her in the hospital.

With a show of hands all voted they believed The Furies were responsible, still no one could explain why Francois knew, or how he was summoned.

"Did you call for him?" E-Z asked. "I mean, how did he know? Which is something I intend to ask him."

"Which brings me right back where we started today," Sam said. "And my question is, why didn't Rosalie know about Francois."

"And how is Little Dorrit?" Sobo inquired.

"I don't know about Francois, but the unicorn was sleeping when I nipped out for some grass this morning."

"Ah, that's good," Lia said.

"Maybe the doctors have an explanation as to why PJ and Arden woke up when they did?" Sam asked.

"That's true, they might, but I don't see how it matters for us. Not really. Main thing is, they are awake and we still don't know if The Furies were responsible for them. However, we do have evidence what they've been doing to other children and one way or another we have to make them pay. And we have to make them stop."

"Maybe the doctors have an explanation as to why PJ and Arden woke up when they did?" Sam asked.

"That's true, they might, but I don't see how it matters for us. Not really. Main thing is, they are awake and we still don't know if The Furies were responsible for them. However, we do have evidence what they've been doing to other children and one way or another we have to make them pay. And we have to make them stop."

"Here! Here!" Charles said, thumping his hand down on the table.

"Can we talk a bit more about Francois," Brandy inquired.

"What if he doesn't want to tell us anything," Charles asked, "unless we accept him as a member of the team?"

"Charles makes a valid point," E-Z said. "I'm prepared to use this as a test with Francois. If he won't tell us what he knows, then maybe he's not meant to be one of us."

"What if he's a really good liar?" Brandy asked. "And some people are excellent liars."

Lia said, "Why don't we do a Zoom call? We can all chat with him, see what he's about and then we can vote on it? I'm already prepared to vote yes."

"No," E-Z said. "I don't want him to know about Charles, Haruto, Lachie or Brandy. All he knows right now is what he can find online."

"And yet," Sam interjected, "Poppet was able to pop into our house."

"Yeah, there's that," E-Z said.

"Plus, he saved Little Dorrit and I – so he knows about her."

""I feel like we're going round and round in circles," Alfred said. "Meanwhile more kids are dying and going into Soul Catchers who belong to others who've died," Alfred said. "I so hoped we'd be further along, after I deciphered the information in the book."

"Wait a minute," E-Z said. "Has anyone seen Hadz and Reiki today?"

None had.

E-Z's phone buzzed. A long text message from PJ and Arden came through:

"Don't ask us how, but we know The Furies are coming your way. And yes, we have a plan. We need to know the minute you see them. Send us a text – and Haruto."

E-Z replied. "What????"

"Trust us," PJ texted.

Both exchanged thumbs up emojis, then he explained the situation to Haruto and the others.

Knowing The Furies were prepared to start the fight now, in their enemy's territory and without their leader Eriel made E-Z feel anxious. They'd lost the element of surprise though, thanks to PJ and Arden.

Still sitting and waiting for them to arrive wasn't the best of strategies.

But they had the advantage now. All they had to do was sit and wait – and hope.

CHAPTER 26
UNEXPECTED VISITORS

ALL WENT ABOUT THEIR business, trying to keep themselves busy while they waited. Then, even though the brick walls, an unescapable stench broke through.

"What is it?" Lia cried, holding her nose closed with her fingers. "I can still smell it!"

Brandy was doing the same with her right and and with her left, she was spraying air freshener around the room which instead of lessening the power of the stink it seemed to make the air thicker and enhance it.

"Let's go outside!" Lachie said. "Maybe it's better out there?" He threw open the door, even though logic told him if the smell was bad inside it had to be worse outside. At first, his senses were fooled and he didn't smell a thing. Was he getting used to it? Were The Furies stink-bombing the inside of the house?

Then he spotted Little Dorrit and Baby, circling above. "It's not any better up here!" Baby said.

"No matter how how we go!" Little Dorrit added.

Then it hit him again, the stink like a slap in the face and for a moment he lost his balance. He spotted the clothesline and pegs, and ran toward them. He clamped one down on his nose, and voila, he couldn't smell a thing. He waved to Little Dorrit and Baby to come down and when they did, he applied the necessary pegs (their noses needed several) until they too could no longer smell the smelly smell.

"Thanks," Little Dorrit and Baby said, as they rose off the ground. "We'll keep a lookout."

Lachie gave them a thumbs up, then noticed a bit of a ruckus going on down the pathway toward the fence was back in the garden. A group of creatures formed a circle, like they were having a meeting. He made his way toward him, as an Owl lifted off a branch and landed on his shoulder.

"Uh, hello," he said, looking into the owl's eyes. "Have we met before?" The owl nodded and then he recognized who it was. It was Sobo. "When you said your superpower was transformation, I didn't think of you like this!"

"Haruto doesn't know," she said. "At least I don't think he remembers me - yet." She flew back to the group of creatures, "Come join us," she said.

Lachie walked among them, being introduced one by one to a deer named Oboe, a racoon named Charlie, a fox named Louise, a bird (Blue Jay) named Lenny and second bird (Cardinal) named Percy.

"We have come, to help," Oboe the deer said, "but we are very afraid of The Furies."

"Let me at'em!" Charlie the raccoon exclaimed. "I'll claw out their eyes."

"And I'll tear out their throats!" Louse the fox cried.

"Whoa! Wait a minute!" Lachie said. "This isn't your fight. Though I appreciate your office to assist, why don't you give us a go first? If we need you to help, I'll whistle and you can come in then?"

"He's right," Sobo said. "Although, he doesn't mean me." She looked at Lachie, to make sure her assumptions were corrected and replied with a nod. "I need to protect my grandson and the others."

Lenny and Percy the two other birds, twittered amongst themselves.

Sobo who had been calm, now began to flap in a most erratic fashion repeating, "Bad things are coming! Terrible things are coming! Dreadful things are coming!"

"Shhh, Sobo," Lachie said, trying to calm her down. "We're ready and they don't know that we know they're coming."

THUMP THUMP THUMP THUMPING

THUMP THUMP THUMP THUMPING

THUMP THUMP THUMP THUMPING

Was the sound the ground under their feet was making, pulsating like a heart trying to break out a chest.

The thumping was followed by drumming.

Then thrumming.

"The Furies are coming!

The Furies are coming!

The Furies are coming!"

While the sky above them churned

And turned.

And burned.

From a brilliant blue to a bloody orangey red.

Neighbours clambered outside, as neighbours do – to see what the smelly smell was all about. Some noisy parkers fainted when their senses were overwhelmed and some brought popcorn out on the porch to eat and watch.

They had no idea what kind of danger was coming their way.

And yet there were clues.

The thrumming whispers.

The thump thump thump thumping.

Still, many did not retreat inside to the safety of their homes.

Instead, they ate their popcorn and drank their sodas, all the while waiting.

GAPING

Without **ESCAPING.**

While the very ground beneath their feet was

THUMP THUMP THUMP THUMPING

THUMP THUMP THUMP THUMPING

THUMP THUMP THUMP THUMPING

Then the thumping was followed by drumming.

Then thrumming.

"The Furies are coming! The Furies are coming! The Furies are coming!"

$$* * *$$

"Let's head outside!" E-Z exclaimed. "And face them head on!" He threw the front door wide open, so it smacked against the wall.

Brandy, Lia, Haruto, Charles and Alfred were behind him, ready to take action the minute they were ordered to do so.

He glanced over his shoulder, to see Sam and Samantha on the way out, "Not you," he said. "The babies need you inside. Leave it to us."

Sam and Samantha retreated.

Now the four soldiers were side by side on the front lawn, waiting. To a stranger they might have looked like a group of children waiting for the school bus to arrive on a normal school day. But this was no normal day. This was Armageddon.

Lia's arms shook and trembled as she searched her mind, opened to her mind, hoping to decipher her superpowers would allow her to access the minds of The Furies. That she'd be able to put herself

out there and find any clues, any information to help her team –
but her mind remained blank.

Alfred said, "I'll fly up onto the roof. See what I can see."

E-Z nodded. "Keep safe. Oh, and see if you can find Lachie and
Sobo." He'd already spotted the unicorn and dragon flying high
above them. He gave them the thumbs up.

A loud whistle, and Baby dove down, Lachie jumped on his
back and a together they joined Alfred on the roof. An owl landed
beside them.

"That's Sobo," Lachie said.

"See anything?" E-Z inquired.

Alfred flapped his wings, "There's a ginormous shelf coming our
way the size of an iceberg but it's moving fast."

E-Z tried to picture it in his mind, but he couldn't because how
the hell were he and his team going to stop such a thing? How?

"It's moving toward us like a a tsunami," Alfred said.

"But it's not made of water," Lachie said. "It looked like it's made
of sand. A sand wave. Carrying three women dressed in black."

A sand wave, yes, now he could picture it. "ETA? I mean
estimated time of arrival?" E-Z asked.

"Hard to tell," Alfred said. "Minutes..."

All the while beneath their feet the ground continued
drumming.

And **thrumming.**

"The Furies are coming! The Furies are coming! The Furies are coming!"

✳✳✳

"GET INSIDE!" E-Z SHOUTED to the nosy neighbours. "Close the doors, lock them. And someone put a notice up on social media. Tell everyone to remain indoors. Tell them not to come outdoors again until they get the all clear from me! Now go!"

SLAM.

SLAM.

Over his shoulder, Alfred, an owl, Lachie, and Baby were looking out, watching as the waved closed the distance between The Furies and his team while Little Dorrit kept a watchful eye from high above.

It was too late to make a plan. Too late to do anything but hope they were ready, as the wind whipped and pushed them around and the earth thumped in synchronicity with their heartbeats.

CRASH.

Behind him, the front door to broke away and flew off its hinges. It bounced and rattled its away along the street before finally resting flat.

Sam stepped out. E-Z turned his chair toward him, not believing his own eyes.

Sam had assembled a costume, or a variety of costumes, creating a superhero character of his own. On his head, was a knight's helmet with the mask flipped up. As he moved forward, it descended and he had to click it back up into place. He'd applied eye black – like baseball players wear to eradicate the glare under his eyes. His chest was puffed out, like he was wearing a bullet proof vest under his shirt, and behind him trailed a long black cape. On his lower half, he wore black jeans, and his favourite pair of running shoes.

The team of superheroes tried not to laugh as he made his way alongside of them, and they noticed his superhero name – SAM THE MAN – was sewed into the fabric across his shoulders.

Little Dorrit dove down, tossed Brandy onto her back. Next, Lachie hopped onto Baby's back and took off. He glanced at the roof. Little Dorrit was no longer there. Alfred and the owl lifted off the roof. All landed alongside of E-Z and the others.

"All for one!" they said. "And one for all!"

"But where is my Sobo?" Haruto asked.

Sobo flew onto his shoulder and immediately he knew it was she. Then she transformed into her human form.

The team of children had seen Sam the Uncle turn into Sam The Man, and Sobo transform from an owl to a grandmother but none of them were phased by it.

Because under their feet the ground continued DRUMMING.

And **THRUMMING.**

But the words had changed.

"The Furies are nearly here.

The Furies are nearly here.

The Furies are nearly here."

$$\ast\ast\ast$$

E -Z AND HIS TEAM watched, as the ginormous sand wave like an ocean liner coming into a harbour drifted in. But this thing ripped through the streets, flattening houses, trees, and every living thing along its way. And it wasn't slowing down.

There wasn't enough time for them to take off, besides, they were stunned by the sheer size of the thing. It did halt, and The Furies reigned over them, their voices shrieking with laughter as they cast their eyes on their foes for the very first time.

"Are they even real?" Tisi inquired. "They look like miniature dolls waiting to be stepped on."

"I see they have a dragon and a unicorn. And a swan. Oh my!" Ali shrieked.

"Remember why we're here," Meg said. "Now you two behave yourself, while I go down and have a conversation with the leader. What was his name again?"

"E-Zed," Tisi shrieked.

"E-Zed," Ali cried.

Together they said the name E-ZED, E-ZED, E-ZED."

"They're calling you E-Z," Brandy said, as she kicked off.

"No!" E-Z cried. "Wait for my order!" But it was too late, Little Dorrit and Brandy were already in flight but they didn't go far, finding a spot on the roof.

E-Z and the rest of the team held their ground.

"What are they waiting for?" Sam asked.

Charles said, "They are hoping their reek will do the job for them. He smiled and everyone laugh. Everyone but Sobo, who transformed back into her owl state, and flew up onto the roof alongside of Brandy and Little Dorrit.

The Furies, who had excellent hearing and who had a plan and were intending to follow it, did not appreciate being the butt of the superhero kids' jokes and one by one took to the air. As they neared, the stink increased as their black robes fluttered in the breeze.

"Catch!" Lachie called out, tossing clothes pegs to each member of the team.

The not so stinky now witches flew closer, so the children below could see them in more detail. In person they were larger than life, literally, due to the snakes which slithered and slid all over those bodies. The forked tongue spitting snakes were accompanied by the sound of whips cracking in an outstanding display of psychological warfare.

It was Meg, as per the original plan who broke the ice, shrieking, "Where's Eriel? We know you have him! Give him to us, NOW."

The high-pitched sound of her shrieking voice made the children cover their ears, as items made of glass such as streetlights, porch lights, windows, and even glass in cupboards shattered for miles and miles.

When he was certain Meg was no longer speaking (since her mouth was closed) E-Z answered, "He's where traitors are kept. So now you can crawl back to whatever hole you three crawled out of!" And when he finished speaking, his lifted off the ground, followed by Alfred, Sobo, Little Dorrit with Brandy Baby with Lachie on board.

"This is our territory. These are our people – and you have no business here. In fact, you have no business here on earth at all. You never did. You don't belong here," E-Z said. "And we're tired of your manipulation. You've overplayed your hand. You've abused your powers. You're despicable. And we're going to make you answer for it."

"What's a little boy like you going to do to us?" Tisi who'd move in beside Meg cried out, "run us over?"

Her shrilled of laughter filled the air, causing the ground under the rest of the team's feet to split into gaps. Lia, Haruto, Charles and Sam huddled together between the gaps for safety.

Meg joined in the name calling fun, "Maybe the swan will tickle us to death? Of course, we can pluck him – and eat him for lunch!"

The non-flying members of the team huddled together even more tightly. Haruto, who could have spun himself away was too frightened to move. Keeping away from the open gaps in the earth which threatened to swallow them up.

"And you little girl," Alli said to Lia. "We tried to melt you in the sun. You got away that time. But what are you going to do to us now? Will you stare at us, with your hands and change us into a statues?"

The Furies' shrieked with laughter again, while the earth below them contracted, like it was trying to give birth to something.

"Bored now," Meg said.

The other two sisters were unusually quiet, like they were uncertain what their next move ought to be.

"Meg flew a little closer to E-Z, with her hands on her hips, "We're wasting our time here! We've not come to battle you today. Not without our leader. All we want to know is, where is he? Let him go. Let him go – now. And we'll save the battle for another day."

"You'd like that wouldn't you!" Alfred shouted.

Which sent Alli into a tizzy.

"Come to me little swanny swanny. The cauldron is waiting for you – you feathered freak!"

"He's a swan, not a goose, you idiot!" Brandy said, as she steered Little Dorrit toward her.

E-Z happy for the distraction received a text from PJ and Arden, and gave Haruto the thumbs up signal.

Haruto spun himself invisible and ran faster than fast to the hospital where he met up with PJ and Arden who were already inside the game waiting. Now they each made a kill. When Haruto arrived, they made two more kills.

The Furies' greed for more children's souls, sent their essences into the game.

"We've got you!" the three-goddesses cried.

"Now!" PJ yelled, as Arden hit SAVE to USB, and when it was saved, he hit EJECT. He closed the USB with masking tape, then put it into an airtight bag.

"Take this to E-Z!" Arden said.

Haruto arrived on the ground, signaled to his grandmother, who grabbed the USB in her beak and took it to E-Z.

PJ texted. "The Furies' essences are in the USB."

E-Z placed the USB safely into his jeans pocket, and the next time he looked at The Furies, the view in Raphael's glasses had altered. The three sisters' bodies were fading in and out, but the snakes were not. It was then he realized what their Achilles Heel was. "The snakes are keeping them alive!" he shouted. "We have to take out the snakes."

Brandy was already close enough to strike Alli. Unfortunately, she was also close enough for Alli's snake to bite her – which it did. She slumped over, and Little Dorrit took off, but it was too late, Brandy was already dead.

"Get her out of here!" E-Z shouted and Little Dorrit took off into the sky sobbing as she went.

"She'll be okay," E-Z said.

"Don't think so," Alli laughed. "Our snakes aren't from this world. If you're bitten by one of these, no matter what powers you have they won't work. But we'll stay around and wait if you want us to? Then when she doesn't come back – we'll blow the rest of your team to smithereens!"

"You bitches!" E-Z exclaimed.

Sobo sprang into action, attacking and pulling out the snake eyes one by one and dropping them to the ground. When she'd finished with Alli, she went on to Meg, then Tisi's. When she finished her task, the grandmother was too exhausted to do anything but land beside her grandson and return to her human form.

"But Sobo," Haruto said, "I want to fight too."

"Let them do the rest," she said. "I'm too weary to carry you."

Sobo, and Haruto watched the rest of the team finish the snakes off.

The Furies opened their mouths and closed them again but no sound emanated from them. Besides being voiceless, and fading, their bodies tried to remain afloat while the blood in their veins drip-dripped down.

E-Z's wheelchair moved about under them, catching the droplets, and blending The Furies blood with the other samples it had collected.

"They're dead," E-Z confirmed, as The Furies empty robes floated like black ghosts toward the ground.

But it wasn't over yet.

✳✳✳

B EHIND E-Z THE SAND wave raised its head, and seeing the punctured eyes all about her – the eyes of all of her children – this mother of all snakes slowly came to life.

Sam, who spotted the movement first shouted, "Look out E-Z!" and when he didn't hear his calls, Lia, Charles, Haruto and Sobo all joined in.

Lachie heard their cries, and saw the snake as her heard slinked its way toward E-Z. He looked into the snake's eyes and said, "NO!"

For a second or two the mother snake stopped moving, and it looked like she heard and understood Lachie's command, then he spotted a flicker in her eye. "Duck E-Z!" he cried, as Baby opened his mouth and shot fire in the direction of E-Z and the mother snake.

E-Z's hair was on fire, and he patted it out, then his chair dropped to the ground.

Baby kept on spewing fire at the giant mother snake until it was burned to a crisp. Instead of the stench which The Furies made, the air was now filled with a foody smell of chicken, such as would be found at any backyard barbecue.

"Uh, thanks Baby and everyone," E-Z said, as he ran his fingers through the middle of his hair. It had taken out the bristle-like part.

"It'll grow back," Sam said, as the ground beneath their feet once again began to

THRUM

AND DRUM

E-Z's wheelchair lifted off the ground of its own volition, and it began to rain down droplets of blood into the craters which had opened up in the ground.

"What's happening?" Alfred asked.

Under him, his wheelchair continued bleeding as jetted him about from place to place. "A little droplet here and a little droplet there," he recited in his mind. On the ground, his team were saying the same words which were going around in his head, "A little droplet here and a little droplet there," then together they finished the poem, "a little little droplet, everywhere," then started all over again. He shook his head...were they all reading his mind?

Beneath their feet, the earth continued.

DRUMMING

THRUMMING.

CONVULSING.

CONTRACTING.

Lia lifted off the ground, opening her arms as wide as they would go with her head slung back and her eyes upon the sky. And above her, the sky tore open. It started to rain, but as they hit the pavement the splotches were red. The sky was crying bloody tears, as Lia swayed and twisted in the air like a stringless marionette.

The others not including Baby and Lachie ran onto the porch to escape the bloody rainfall, unable to do anything about Lia who was still suspended and in a trance.

"We'll make sure she doesn't fall," E-Z said, "the rest of you take cover."

PULSING.

PUSHING.

Then there was **lightning.**

Followed by **thunder.**

As the archangel Michael broke through the barrier and flew down until he was near to E-Z.

"I understand you have the situation under control, Michael said.

"Yes, The Furies' essences are in this USB."

"Toss it to me," Michael said.

Like he was throwing a baseball to second base, E-Z fired the USB in the direction of Michael, who reached out and caught it and encased it in ice. "I Eriel will have company," Michael said. "They'll all remained on ice for the rest of eternity. Oh, and by the way, well done everyone!" Then as quickly as he had come, he flew away.

"What about Lia?" E-Z shouted, but Michael did not reply.

The earth began to pulse and twist even though The Furies were no longer on it, and the blood was no longer flowing from the sky or his wheelchair.

Lia was still floating with her eyes directed at the sky, as it churned itself from bloody tears to blue, and beneath their feet the earth craters were healed with grass, trees flowers.

Then everything went quiet, as Lia, still in a trance floated back down to the ground. Prostrate on the ground, with her arms still wide open, she felt the grass on her back and she smiled with exhaustion, as she shrunk in size and returned to her true age which was nine and a half years old.

"Are you okay?" E-Z asked, as the fox, the blue jay, the racoon, the cardinal, and the deer gathered round.

Lia opened her eyes, and she could see out of them. She looked at her hands and they were as they used to be.

"I'm good," she said, as Lachie helped her up.

Sam noticing immediately that his daughter's clothes didn't fit her anymore. He removed his superhero cape and wrapped it around her shoulders.

"Thanks Dad," Lia said.

It was the first time she'd ever called him that and he never felt so proud as a tear ran down his cheek.

✳✳✳

T HE BLUE IN THE sky seemed brighter, like the stars were blinking their eyes even though it was daytime and the grass on the ground seemed to dance in the sun rays like it contained diamond dew.

Neither E-Z nor any member of his team could speak. No one wanted to break the silence, or disturb the beauty they were witness to.

WHISPER.

WHISPER WHISPER.

WHISPERING WHISPERED WHISPERS.

The leaves, blowing in the wind. Making a human-like sound. But it wasn't the wind, it was the voice of children around the world being reborn.

Those who had been taken by The Furies, pushed their bodies out of the ground, and found their voices had returned.

The children relearned how to walk, run, or crawl, and their cries echoed around the world:

"I want my mommy!" the reborn but soul less bodies of the children screamed.

"I want my daddy!" those resurrected children cried out in one voice:

"WAH, WAH, WAH!"

"WAH, WAH, WAH!"

"WAH, WAH, WAH!"

The soulless little ones moved to edges, travelling to places, their movements faster than the speed of light as they continued to wail:

"I want my mommy!"

"I want my daddy!"

"WAH, WAH, WAH!"

"WAH, WAH, WAH!"

"WAH, WAH, WAH!"

In Death Valley, where the Soul Catchers were kept and stored,

POP

POP

The doors flew open, like arms, and the souls exited, searching for the bodies in which they were still meant to be and they followed the cries of the children.

"I want my mommy!"

"I want my daddy!"

"WAH, WAH, WAH!"

"WAH, WAH, WAH!"

"WAH, WAH, WAH!"

The souls flew from child to child. Searching for the home in which it belonged. It was like watching children playing a game of tag, as each soul came upon and entered the body in which it had been born. As the souls and bodies became one again.

SHHHHHHH.

For a moment in time, the little ones were happy children once again and sounds of delight filled the air.

Back in Death Valley, Hadz and Reiki redirected the homeless souls across the world who'd been in hiding since they had no Soul Catchers of their own. One by one, souls entered and the earth began to heal itself.

Samantha came out of the house, carrying her babies Jack and Jill in her arms while singing softly to them, "Hush little baby don't you cry."

POP.

POP.

Hadz and Reiki appeared, "We did it!"

E-Z and his team threw their arms around each other. They cried, they laughed. Then they cried again, for the loss of one of their team. For the loss of one of their own: Brandy.

Lia's phone pinged. It was a message from Brandy, "I arrived in the shopping centre – again! I hope everyone is okay and we beat those witches!"

"Brandy's alive!" Lia explained, then she texted back, "We sure did! I'll fill you in on the details later."

"AHRHHRGHHH!" Charles Dickens cried. His body was shaking and trembling. When it stopped he was in a trance with an expressionless look on his face and his outstretched with palms facing up.

"Is he getting my hand eyes?" Lia inquired.

As a book – the biggest hardcover volume they'd ever seen - dropped from the sky and landed in Charles' arms the very force of it nearly knocking him off his feet. Charles steadied himself, as the massive book opened itself, flipping its own pages until a voice from inside the book rang out:

"I am the Alternate Worlds Travelogue."

Although the voice was coming from inside the book, Charles Dickens' lips moved in synchronicity with every word while in the background the cries of children still rang out:

"WAH, WAH, WAH!"

"WAH, WAH, WAH!"

"WAH, WAH, WAH!"

"I want my mommy!"

"I want my daddy!"

"WAH, WAH, WAH!"

"WAH, WAH, WAH!"

"WAH, WAH, WAH!"

"I'm hungry!"

"I'm thirsty!"

The children who once lived nearest to E-Z's house, marched side by side toward it.

"Hear me now!" The Alternate Worlds Travelogue soliloquized.

"This is a onetime only offer.

If you are chosen, you must choose.

One time only, win or lose.

Don't let this opportunity, get away.

For it will not happen again, on any other day."

The pages flipped forward, then back. Forward then back. The flipping stopped on a chapter. A chapter entitled Alfred. And there were photos, of him, with his family. All older. All healthy and well. He was no longer Alfred the trumpeter swan in the photos. He was Alfred the father, the husband, the man.

With tears in his eyes, Alfred glanced at E-Z. The look they shared between them said everything. He had to go. E-Z nodded.

Then Alfred turned to Lia. She nodded also, knowing that he had to go.

Alfred the trumpeter swan stepped into the chapter bearing his name and transformed back into a man. And from within the pages of The Alternate Worlds Travelogue, he waved to his friends.

Now the pages of the Alternate Worlds Travelogue reset to the beginning of the book. The pages shuffled, over and over again, forwards, and back, back, and forwards eventually stopping at a new chapter. A chapter named for Lachie.

In the photo, Lachie was an infant. His parents were taking him home from the hospital. The infant in the photo wore a hospital bracelet revealing that Lachie's real name was Andrew.

"No, thank you," Lachie said. "Baby and I will be going home soon."

The Alternate Worlds Travelogue slammed itself shut with such force that Charles nearly fell over. He recovered, and moments later the book resumed flipping. Backwards, forwards. Shuffling pages like a deck or cards until it landed on the chapter called Haruto. In the photo, he was with his mother and father.

"No thank you," Haruto immediately said. He took Sobo's hand into his and said to Lachie, "Mind dropping us off in Japan on your way home?"

Lachie nodded, "Glad for the company."

Flames shot out of the book this time before it closed, and Charles nearly dropped it.

The children's unanswered cries continued, growing louder as they neared E-Z's home:

"I want my mommy!"

"I want my daddy!"

"I'm hungry!"

"I'm thirsty!"

"WAH, WAH, WAH!"

"WAH, WAH, WAH!"

"WAH, WAH, WAH!"

Charles closed his eyes.

"Is that it? E-Z inquired.

"What about us?" Lia asked.

Charles' arms began to shake. Like the weight of the book was pressing down upon his arms. Then the book slammed shut, with such an intensity that he stumbled forward and sat down. He crossed one leg over the other, and cradled the book against his chest.

It flew open again as did Charles eyes, and once again the pages moved about, like seagrasses on the ocean floor. It slammed shut again. Then flipped over onto its back. In the centre of the book, a frame appeared. At first it was empty, like it was waiting for something. Then it flickered as a movie began.

A baseball game had already started in Dodger Stadium. The Dodgers were playing The Brewers. And E-Z Dickens was the catcher. He was behind the plate and playing like a pro. In the stands were his parents, just over the dugout, cheering him on.

EARTH PAUSE.

For a few seconds, the sunlight was blocked as Ophaniel burst into the sky and made her way toward them.

"E-Z, I just wanted to tell you, before you make your decision, that whatever you decide to do, or not to do will have consequences to others."

"Like what?" he asked, not taking his eye off the framed version of himself and his parents, even though they were no longer moving in it.

"Think about the accident...what wouldn't have happened, in the world, if your parents had never died? If you had never lost the use of your legs?"

He glanced in the direction of his Uncle Sam, then at Samantha, Lia, and the twins. Without the accident, none of them would have met. The twins would never have been born.

"If I decide to go and live out my dream, what will happen here?"

"It's a risk you would have to take, and an answer I cannot give you. But I do know this, you're the catalyst and the glue."

"Okay, thanks for letting me know."

EARTH RESUME

Ophaniel departed.

"Uh, no thank you," E-Z said.

He watched as he and his parents faded away. The screen went blank. The frame disappeared and the book began to rise. Up, up, out of Charles' arms.

Charles stood like he was still holding it. Staring ahead at nothing.

When it was far above them, the book burst into flames. It sizzled and created a stink before its remnants were small enough to be lifted by the wind. And the Alternate Worlds Travelogue was no more.

Charles returned to himself as the children arrived onto E-Z's street en masse.

"I want my mommy!"

"I want my daddy!"

"I'm hungry!"

"I'm thirsty!"

"WAH, WAH, WAH!"

"WAH, WAH, WAH!"

"WAH, WAH, WAH!"

"May I tell them a story?" Charles asked.

"It couldn't hurt," Lia said.

Charles began to retell the tale of The Three Boulders. The children stopped moving, halted their cries as they hung on his each and every single word – until he came to an abrupt stop.

"Oh, bother!" he cried, noticing every bit of him was fading in and out like the earth was having trouble transmitting his signal.

"Wait!" E-Z said. "Any advice you have for a fellow writer?"

"There are books in which the backs and covers are the best parts – don't let yours be one of those. I shall miss you all!"

Some say at that exact moment, a ray of light came down, lifted him off the ground and carried Charles Dickens off into the sky. Some say, he rode away on Little Dorrit and neither of them were ever seen again. All they knew for certain was that Charles Dickens left them on that day and was never seen again.

"WAH, WAH, WAH!"

"WAH, WAH, WAH!"

"WAH, WAH, WAH!"

FIZZLE POP

A Soul Catcher arrived. It threw its door open, and shot firecrackers into the air.

Some of the babies were frightened by the noise and some loved it, in all cases they stopped crying.

As it shot colours into the air, they melted together to say the following:

COME OUT COME OUT

WHEREVER YOU ARE!

"What does it want?" E-Z asked. "Or should I say, WHO does it want?"

"Is it me?" Sobo asked.

"No, it's for me," a voice behind them said. It was the voice of Rosalie.

All turned toward something, expecting to see a ghost or a spirit, but what they saw was neither of those two things. It was Rosalie's essence...that's all they knew.

"Goodbye dear Rosalie!" Sobo called.

It was quite a sendoff for dear Rosalie's essence, with E-Z and his team shouting, waving, throwing kisses and cheering for her. It was a true celebration of everything she'd meant to them, as their dear friends stepped into her Soul Catcher and it flew away.

Now that Charles was gone the children resumed their cries,

"WAH, WAH, WAH!"

"WAH, WAH, WAH!"

"WAH, WAH, WAH!"

In the background, there was a new sound. The sound of feet, many feet, running – fast.

As they flowed into E-Z's street, the mommies and daddies and the children were reunited with their loved ones, and this reunification occurred throughout the earth.

"Bravo!" E-Z said to his team.

They waved good-bye as Lachie, Baby, Haruto and Sobo flew away.

Now the only ones left were E-Z and Lia.

ZAP!

First Poppet arrived.

BONJOUR!

Followed by Francois.

"Ah, we're too late," he said. "We've missed everything!"

From inside the house, Samantha's cries were heard. "Oh no, something is happening with the babies!"

Everyone ran inside to the babies nursery. Jack and Jill were sound asleep.

Sam put his arm around his wife. "They look fine to me," he whispered.

"But they are not fine!" Samantha said.

"It'll be okay," Sam said.

"They look fine to me too," E-Z said.

"You just wait," Samantha said. "Just wait and you'll see. I wouldn't have cried out unless..." she teetered and tottered like she might fall down.

All watched and waited. Nothing happened for ten, fifteen, twenty, or even thirty minutes.

Then suddenly, something did happen.

A yellow light and a green light emanated from Jack and Jill's tiny bodies.

"Hadz? Reiki?" E-Z exclaimed.

POP.

POP.

Jack and Jill sat up, like older babies would be able to do. Which Jack and Jill could not yet do.

Samantha fainted, while Sam caught her.

"What the heck are you two doing?" E-Z demanded. "Get out of there – now!"

Hadz said, "As a reward we asked to be human."

"Reiki said, "And we needed bodies."

"Oh brother," E-Z said, as there was a knock on the front door.

"Anyone home?" PJ and Arden inquired.

EPILOGUE

E-Z typed in the words: **THE END**. Satisfied with his accomplishment of completing a series of four books, he closed his laptop.

"Hurry up E-Z!" a man behind him shouted.

E-Z pulled off his catcher's mask and had a look around. He was behind the plate, catching for the Los Angeles Dodgers. The ump was brushing off the plate. He stood up, and made his way into the dugout since he was the last player off the field.

He recognized a few of the players, as he moved along the dugout following closely behind them.

He ran his fingers through his hair, which was all blond. It was shorter, and a closer cut than he'd ever had before. And he was taller, definitely over 6 ft 5.

What the heck was going on? Was he asleep? He pinched himself. It hurt.

"You're on deck, E-Z!" the batting coach shouted.

He found a monitor and checked out his reflection. He looked at himself, like he was a stranger.

"Earth to E-Z," his coach said.

"Sorry, Coach," E-Z said, as he made his way toward the dugout gear hangar. His bat was labeled, as was all the rest of his gear. He put it on and stepped into the on-deck circle.

He adjusted his elbow pads, then readied himself for the first pitch. Along with his teammate at the plate, he took a couple of practice swings. As he waited movement in the stands behind the dugout caught his eye. His mother and father.

"Go, get'em son!" his dad shouted.

He gave his parents the thumbs up, then watched as his teammate singled and made it safely to first base.

E-Z stepped into the batter's box, called time, stepped back out again, and took a few deep breaths.

Pull yourself together, he told himself. *I don't want to let the team down. Focus. Concentrate.*

He raised his arm to let the umpire know he was ready, then returned to the plate.

"Come on E-Z!" his mother called.

He concentrated and watched as the first pitch went by. Probably over one hundred miles an hour. He prepared himself for the second pitch. Swung and missed. His teammate stole a base and landed safely at second.

This is too much. I'm not ready. I have to wake up. I have to wake up – NOW.

The second pitch flew by. He swung but did not connect. The third pitch came in, and he connected with it. He watched as his teammate tried to make it to third, but was thrown out. He nearly made it to first on time, but the other team earned a double play. With two out, he went back to the dugout to put on his catching gear.

"You'll get'em next time!" his father said.

Even though he didn't make it on base, he was in his dream. Living out his dream. But how? He'd refused the offer from the Alternate Worlds Travelogue.

Get me out of here! I don't want it this way! Where's Uncle Sam? Where's Lia? Where are the twins?

His head was filled with laughter as he dropped to the ground, and continued falling. Until he landed with a thump on a wooden floor, in a cabin, or a shack. Within seconds of his landing, it burst into flames.

Across the room sat a little girl. At first, he thought it was Lia, but this girl had red hair. He tried to wake her, but she didn't budge.

Behind him, the front door was thrown from its hinges. A dark, shrouded figure entered, with a shorter hooded figure. Between the two of them they carried the girl outside.

"Help me!" he cried.

"Help yourself!" a woman's voice, the taller of the two figures said, as the walls began to crash all around him.

He was back in the stadium, on his back on the ground looking up into his parents' eyes.

"You'll be okay," they cooed.

Thank you!

Dears readers,

Well, we made it to the end of the E-Z Dickens Series. I sure hope you liked reading it as much as I enjoyed writing it.

Since you've been with me throughout this series, my final THANK YOU is to you, my readers. You're awesome!

As always, Happy Reading!

Cathy

About The Author

Cathy McGough is a Canadian author whose work spans children's literature; young adult fiction; literary fiction; psychological thrillers; poetry; short stories and non-fiction. She lives and writes in Ontario, Canada with her family.

Also by:

YA

A Mathematical State of Grace Complete Series

NON-FICTION

103 Fundraising Ideas For Parent Volunteers With Schools and Teams (3RD PLACE BEST REFERENCE 2016 METAMORPH PUBLISHING)

FICTION

Interviews With Legendary Writers From Beyond (2ND PLACE BEST LITERARY 2016 METAMORPH PUBLISHING)

Thirteen Short Stories

POETRY

PAINTING WITH WORDS

+ Children's Books.

www.ingramcontent.com/pod-product-compliance
Lightning Source LLC
Chambersburg PA
CBHW030807210726

48290CB00002B/460